Envy
and the
Geek

NATALIE FALKENWRATII

BENTON HOUSE PUBLISHING

Benton House Publishing

bentonhousepublishing.com

This is a work of fiction. Names, characters, business, events and incidents are the products of the author's imagination. Any resemblance to actual persons, living or dead, or actual events is purely coincidental.

ISBN 978-1-952057-11-3 (Paperback)

ISBN 978-1-952057-12-0 (eBook)

For more information about the author and
upcoming books, please visit
nataliefalkenwrath.com

Dedicated to Minicon and all of fandom.

Prologue

High School Bites Fanfic

Francesca knew what was in her heart—that cold, unbeating heart. Years ago, frightened by the power of her feelings for Alessia and out of fear of rejection, Francesca had walked away. She'd left Alessia alone when Alessia had needed her the most. It was the worst mistake of Francesca's eternal life. Would Alessia forgive her?

"Please say something," Francesca pleaded.

Alessia bit her lip, showing off one small white fang. The air hung thick with silent tension.

"Please, Alessia. Tell me we can be friends once more."

Alessia looked hard at Francesca—her ice blue eyes seemed to penetrate her, sending a chill through Francesca's already cold body. "But it's not just my friendship you want, is it?" Alessia narrowed her eyes at her once best friend.

Slowly Francesca shook her head. Alessia knew her too well—they'd been undead together for a hundred years. And Francesca owed her the truth. "I love you, Alessia."

The night air felt as still as death while Francesca waited for Alessia to respond. Alessia was biting her lips again, her sharp fang penetrated the soft skin of her bottom lip, and a dot of blood appeared, like a dewdrop on a rose. Francesca licked her own lips, hungry for the taste of her best friend and the woman she loved.

"Alessia, if you don't feel the way I do I... I understand, but I had to tell you I couldn't live—"

"You don't get to live. Neither of us does." Alessia finally spoke.

Francesca's heart sank. She looked at her feet.

"But we do exist," Alessia continued. She took a step forward so that the toes of her tall boots touched Francesca's. Francesca looked up. Alessia was looking at her with such tenderness. "And I don't want to exist without you," she said.

Chapter 1:
Harmony

Harmony Adler wiggled in her seat, making her chair roll side to side on the cement floor of her basement office. The office was large—she shared it with two fellow post-docs—but the room's tiny windows only allowed the barest hint of natural light to enter the room—not nearly enough to ascertain the time of day. Harmony glanced up at the windows, then down at her watch. With a sigh she turned back down at her computer screen. Harmony was having a hard time concentrating on her work. The data she was entering was vital to her experiment, but her mind wasn't on physics; it was on her very favorite science fiction convention: JanCon.

Once upon a time, JanCon had been held in January. It had been the off-season sibling to another larger convention. Or so she'd been told; Harmony didn't know that version of JanCon. All that she'd ever experienced was JanCon as it currently existed: an independent volunteer-run convention held in the spring. An annual event where hundreds of fans of science fiction and fantasy—literature and media—gathered as a community to celebrate their shared interests. It was like a giant weekend-long geek party, and Harmony could not wait to get there.

Once the last dataset had been entered, Harmony shot off an email to her colleagues letting them know the task was complete. Then she happily tapped her email closed with an exaggerated *poke* of her finger. She spun around in her chair and popped up with a flourish.

"That's it. I am calling it. My weekend starts *now*," she announced to her officemates, Dean and Joe. Her announcement was met only by the quiet whirring of the fan that kept the room at a bearable temperature. Harmony twisted around on the balls of her feet, looking back and forth between her two coworkers, both engrossed in their computer screens—headphones on, expressions blank. Harmony shook her head, making her orange-gold curls whip across her face.

"My weekend starts *now*!" she called out again, putting her hands on her hips and thrusting out her chest in a dramatic pose. To her right, Dean lifted an eyebrow and pulled the earbud out of one ear.

"You're leaving?" he asked.

"Yup!" she chirped back, chin held high.

"Okay then." He began to put the earbud back in, but Harmony bounced over and leaned against his desk. He stopped and looked up at her expectantly.

"Did I tell you where I'm going this weekend? I'm going to JanCon!" she gushed, not waiting for an answer.

"Yeah, you told me. More than once." Dean returned the earbud to his ear and turned his eyes back to his computer. Harmony gave him a quick faux-angry scowl before once more breaking out into a wide grin. She hopped over to Joe, her converse sneakers squeaking on the polished cement as she did. She leaned over and waved at him until he took off his headphones.

"What's up?" Joe asked.

"Just saying goodbye for the weekend. I'm headed out to JanCon!" she said.

Joe gave her a friendly smile and leaned back in his squeaky black office chair. "Fun. What's the theme this year?" he asked. Joe had some experience with science fiction conventions, so at least he was willing to talk to her about it.

"*Vampires in Space*," Harmony said with a soft snort. "I think they were reaching a little because they wanted to appease both guests of honor."

"Yeah? Who are the guests of honor?" he asked, swiveling back and forth in his chair.

"There's some Hugo Award-winning author, Charlie McGillicuddy or something—I haven't read his stuff," Harmony said dismissively before clasping her hands together and clutching them to her chest. "And *Christina Darlington*." She sighed and closed her eyes, picturing the beautiful blonde actress who had been the object of her affection for so many years.

"Who?" Joe asked.

Harmony opened her eyes. Joe was looking at her blankly, his head tilted to one side. *Of course, he wouldn't recognize her name out of context.* "Do you remember the TV show High School Bites? It was about teen vampires. It aired for a few years back when I was in middle school." Harmony had been massively addicted to that show. She'd recorded every episode and re-watched them a hundred times each.

"Yeah, I think I vaguely remember something like that," Joe said, nodding slowly.

"Well, Christina Darlington played one of the vampires, Alessia," Harmony explained.

"I didn't watch it, sorry," Joe apologized with a shrug. Harmony wasn't surprised. High School Bites had its own cult following but was never wildly successful.

Harmony had started watching High School Bites at age fourteen—around the same time she'd begun examining her attractions to others. She hadn't started dating yet, but based on available data, she'd suspected that she might be bisexual. When she developed a *massive* crush on Alessia, that suspicion was confirmed. Harmony Adler liked girls; she *really* liked girls. *Especially* Christina Darlington.

Over the years, her feelings turned toward real, datable humans. But when Christina came out as gay a couple of years ago, Harmony's dormant teenage crush had roared back to life. And this weekend Harmony would meet the object of her affection—her first-ever girl crush—in person. Harmony sighed again. It was like a dream come true.

"She's so beautiful, tall and blonde and *fierce*." Harmony's heart fluttered in her chest. Alessia was so *hot* with her tiny little fangs and even tinier little outfits, and years later the actress who had played her was still drop-dead gorgeous—at least from what Harmony could tell via Google.

Harmony had read everything about Christina she could find online. She was a year older than Harmony. Born in the LA area, she had begun her acting career as a small child, appearing in bit parts and commercials until she landed her big break—teen vampire sweetheart Alessia. Christina hadn't appeared in any major roles since High School Bites. These days she mostly worked the convention circuit.

Rumor had it that Christina would often get quite *close* with her fans; several women online claimed to have hooked up with the actress at various conventions. Harmony's imagination ran wild with the idea that such a thing could happen to her. Whether or not the rumors were true, Harmony eagerly anticipated meeting Christina.

"I'm so excited!" Harmony squealed. She put on her backpack and pulled the straps until it settled evenly and securely on her back. "Okay, well, I'm out of here. See you Tuesday!"

With one last perky wave at Joe and Dean, Harmony skipped out the door. She bounded up the stairs and burst out of the front doors of the research center. The sun was hidden behind gray clouds that covered the sky like a downy blanket. But the gloomy weather couldn't dampen Harmony's bright mood. She skipped merrily down the sidewalk toward the bike rack—both her heavy backpack and large breasts bouncing against her body in protest of her overly-enthusiastic movements. She ignored the discomfort and quickly closed the short distance between the building and her trusty bicycle.

Harmony whistled the theme song to High School Bites as she carefully unlocked her bike, checked the tire pressure—*good enough*—and secured her helmet. The commute back to her house was usually a forty-seven-minute ride, but Harmony was so excited she made it in forty-one. Her chest was heaving as she climbed off her bike and wheeled it into the detached garage. She walked back across the tiny lawn toward the small 1900s craftsman-style home she shared with her roommate, Shay.

The screen door banged shut behind her, and she stood still just inside the door. It took a minute for Harmony's eyes to adjust. "It's fucking dark in here," she quoted aloud to herself with a giggle. She kicked off her shoes and slid along the hardwood floor in her socks, gliding down the hall to her room. Harmony flipped on the light.

God, my room is such a disaster. Harmony was a perfectly tidy roommate in communal spaces. But her own room was always somewhere between a little messy and a total when-did-the-tornado-hit catastrophe. She'd packed for the convention last night. Now her blue duffle bag sat, stuffed, in the middle of the room, surrounded by abject chaos.

Harmony wriggled out of the blue polo shirt she'd worn to work. *Should I shower?* She looked at herself in the mirror hanging on the back of her closet door. Her curls had been smashed down by her helmet and blown into a frizzy tangle by the wind. It wasn't a pretty sight. Harmony sniffed her underarms. *Yup, I definitely need a shower.* There was no reason she needed to play into *all* the geek stereotypes. She could at least try to look and smell like a civilized human being.

Harmony stripped off the rest of her clothing and again examined herself in the mirror. There was a sheen of sweat on her chest; she ran her fingers down her sternum, between her breasts, and across her pale abdomen. She rested her hands on her hips. Harmony considered herself reasonably attractive; her curves were soft, and her face was cute, with a button nose, rosy cheeks, and full lips. *But am I pretty enough to get Christina's attention?*

Harmony never had trouble finding people interested in hooking up at con. But those were other fans—ordinary, nerdy people. This weekend Harmony had her sights set on a *star*. Do actresses hook up with "reasonably attractive" women or only tv-pretty types? Harmony wasn't sure, but it never hurt to try. *I should shave. Gotta put my best self forward if I'm going to get some this weekend.* She hoped that "some" would be coming from Christina, but either way, Harmony would have fun at the convention. *Worst case scenario, I don't get to have any sex, and all I wasted was a few extra minutes.*

Once washed and shaved, Harmony dressed in jeans, a geeky t-shirt, and her lucky unicorn socks. After a quick lunch of peanut butter and jelly, she packed up her car and hit the road.

The convention was being held in a large hotel in Chicago. It wasn't far away, as the crow flies. But the crow didn't have to deal with traffic. Besides which, Harmony was coming from the ass-opposite end of the city. She listened to National Public Radio as her red

Corolla crawled towards JanCon. The drive itself was draining, but the moment the hotel came into view Harmony's energy surged again.

The hotel itself wasn't much to write home about—just another mid-range city hotel run by a large corporate chain—but it was *home*, a home she shared with the fannish community of JanCon. Although Harmony had only been going to the convention for five years, the con regulars had quickly become like a second family to her, especially the group of volunteers who ran the convention.

When Harmony stepped through the hotel's revolving doors, she couldn't help but grin. Tingles of excitement made the hairs on the back of her neck stand on end. She glanced around the wide, plain lobby, with its simple furniture and neutral color scheme. There wasn't much evidence to indicate that a convention was about to begin, aside from a few posters stuck to the walls with blue painter's tape. But she'd expected as much; she'd arrived early to help get things set up and ready for when the hoards descended the next day.

Harmony walked up to the front desk and dropped her bag with a loud *thud*. The woman behind the desk jumped and looked up at Harmony with a sour expression. She was middle-aged with a frilly blouse, hairspray-shiny black curls, and pinched lips with poorly applied pink lipstick. All her makeup looked like it had been slapped on hastily with an oversize painted brush. And she was wearing enough perfume to make Harmony's eye water.

"I'm checking in," Harmony said, trying her very best not to recoil at the smell. The woman took Harmony's information and typed it into the computer. Her long nails clicked loudly on the cheap keyboard as she pulled up her reservation.

"How many keys would you like?" the woman asked.

"Three, please," Harmony responded. She always got three keys: a primary key, a backup key, and a hook-up key. The desk lady raised an over-plucked eyebrow at Harmony.

"And you're the only occupant?" she asked.

"Unless I get lucky." Harmony winked at her. "Oh, and can you put them in separate little envelope things?"

The woman pursed her lips, shaking her head in obvious disapproval, but she handed over three keycards, each in its own paper sleeve. *Judge all you want, stink-lady. I'm here to have fun.*

"You are in room fifteen-thirty-two; the elevators are down the hall and to the left. Please enjoy your stay."

"Thanks!" Harmony picked up her bag again, hefting it over her shoulder, and walked toward the elevator. She stepped inside and hit the button. When their shiny metal doors opened on her floor, Harmony shuffled quickly to the door labeled 1532 and let herself in.

The room felt both familiar and unremarkable. A single king-sized bed made up with white linens was flanked by two small nightstands. A desk, dresser, and an uncomfortable-looking chair sat around the periphery of the room. Harmony tossed her duffle onto the bed and kicked off her shoes. She preferred to walk around the hotel in her socks. She quickly used the bathroom, double-checked that she didn't have peanut butter and jelly on her face, and was back out the door.

The primary convention spaces were on the sprawling bottom two floors, broken up into ballrooms and convention halls, connected by wide corridors to a couple dozen hotel suites with patios and balconies. A large poster board welcomed Harmony to JanCon. "Follow the red line," it read, pointing to a stripe of crimson tape running along the floor. The trail snaked through the hotel, leading Harmony to the convention registration desk. Harmony didn't *need* the direction, but it was fun to follow along nonetheless.

When she arrived, Harmony waved vigorously at her friend Mac. He was currently staffing the desk where pre-registered con-goers stopped to pick up their badges. She hadn't seen Mac in ages. He was tall and long-faced, with shiny black hair pulled back into a low ponytail. He was wearing this year's JanCon t-shirt and black jeans.

He raised a hand back at her in greeting. "Hey there, Harmony," he said.

"Hi! How's it going?" Harmony asked, skipping up to stand across the table from Mac.

"I haven't been here long, but so far so good," he answered. "Want me to get you your badge?"

"Yes, please!" she replied with a grin. "Need any help working the reg desk?"

"Naw, it's pretty slow yet. I know the art room and the consuite both need volunteers though," Mac said as he retrieved her regular badge along with a second one designating her as a volunteer.

Consuite or art room? Working in the consuite would likely mean prepping veggie trays, mixing soup, or hauling ice. She wrinkled her nose. She disliked working with food. It gave her flashbacks to her college years when she'd been forced to work in the school cafeteria to help pay tuition. That was ages ago, but the sight of plastic gloves still brought back vivid memories of slopping out food and wiping up grease while her classmates chattered on the other side of the serving counter. *No, thank you.*

"I guess I'll head over to the art room then," Harmony said.

"Okay." Mac pulled out a pocket program—a small booklet containing all the vital convention information—and handed it to Harmony. "Look for Helen; she's the art chair this year," he said.

"Okie dokie." Harmony examined the program schedule. The Art show didn't officially open until the following day. She wondered how many artists had already brought their works to showcase and sell at the convention. They would need help locating their designated places and setting up as they arrived. *That could be fun.* Harmony began in that direction but she didn't get far.

"Who's that cute girl walking toward me?" Harmony's friend Chris called out with a wide grin.

"Hi!" Harmony bounded up to him, and he opened his arms, wrapping her in a bone-crushing embrace. Chris was short and barrel-chested with shaggy blonde hair and an ever-present five o'clock shadow. He was sweet, and flirty, and he never missed the chance to hug or snuggle a "cute girl." Harmony enjoyed that about him; he was an excellent cuddler—once you got past the initial squeeze-you-to-death hug.

"How's it going?" Harmony asked when Chris dropped his arms from around her.

"Let me tell you, this new hotel management has been so wonderful," Chris said. "This might be the smoothest running JanCon ever."

"Yeah? How so?" Harmony asked, thinking back to the not-so-friendly front desk clerk.

Chris held out his hand to count his praises out on his fingers. "One: they actually got the room blocks organized as requested. Two: they are letting the con put up signs across the *entire* hotel. Three: they gave us a new floorplan that's actually accurate—it's on the pocket program."

"Yeah, I saw." Harmony nodded. "I thought it seemed more to scale."

"And four," Chris continued. "They aren't bitching about the consuite serving food *and* alcohol. Speaking of, are you going to come up and work in the consuite? I could use an extra pair of hands, and you're pretty easy on the eyes, Harmony." Chris waggled his eyebrows at her.

Harmony winced. She didn't want to go to the consuite. But Chris was her friend, and she didn't feel like she could really say no. "Sure. But don't make me deal with anything... pungent, alright?"

"So you'll make the fish chowder then?" Chris teased.

Harmony shook her head, her curls swinging violently, and stuck out her tongue at Chris. "Yuck. You know, on second thought, I think I'll head to the art room…" She turned away from him.

"Aw, come on." Chris took her hand, spinning her back around. "You can help me set up the bar."

With an *okay-you-got-me* grin Harmony let Chris lead her to the consuite and bar—two large adjoining suites that served as the convention's hub for all things consumable. There, volunteers would serve up food and drinks all con long. The space was a flurry of activity, although it wasn't officially open yet. All the people buzzing around were volunteers like Harmony. Some set up tables, covering them with linens and littering them with snacks. Others were hanging strings of lights and other decorations to give the rooms a party-like vibe.

Chris put Harmony to work filling the bathtub with beer and ice. She buried the cans as deeply as she could and stirred some water into the ice to speed up the heat transfer to better cool the warm beers. By the time she was done, her hands were numb with cold. Goosebumps covered her skin, and she shivered as she walked back out to where Chris was mixing the classic convention punch.

"Done," she announced triumphantly.

"Is it cold in here, or are you just happy to see me?" Chris asked.

Harmony looked down; her nipples were so hard they could cut glass. She folded her arms across her chest and shoved her hands in her armpits. She smirked at Chris. "Don't flatter yourself." She shivered again. "Brrr. I am done with ice. You, sir, owe me a drink."

"Here, be the first to sample this batch of con punch," Chris said as he filled a red solo cup with vodka and the peach-pink concoction. Harmony hopped up to sit on the counter beside him. She reached out for the drink, but Chris withdrew the cup from her reach.

"Actually, don't sit on the counter; I need to prep garnishes," he said. With a sigh, Harmony jumped back off again. Chris watched her; a mischievous smile curled the corner of his mouth. "You know, why don't you hop back up there again," he said.

Harmony narrowed her eyes at him as she snatched the drink from his hand. "You just want to watch my boobs bounce again," she chided.

"Can you blame me?" he grinned.

She rolled her eyes dramatically and sighed. If he hadn't been her good friend, she might have been legitimately annoyed, but she didn't mind that type of banter coming from Chris. "I suppose not," she said. "I'm a pretty big fan of boobs myself, you know."

Harmony took a sip of her punch and glanced around the consuite. *There is a distinct lack of boobs in here today,* she thought. JanCon usually had a lot of female volunteers, but they were a little thin on the ground at the moment.

"I hope I get to spend a little quality time with ta-tas other than my own this weekend, though," Harmony mused, patting one of her breasts.

"If you need somebody to spend time with yours, I volunteer as tribute," Chris offered.

"Nope, sorry." Harmony shook her head. "I'm saving myself for the ladies this year—one lady in particular."

"Oh yeah? Who?"

"Christina Darlington," Harmony said, slurping down more of the sweet beverage. Con punch was so good when the proportions of each ingredient—juice, soda, and vodka—were correct. And Chris had mixed it perfectly.

"The actress? You're looking to hook up with a guest of honor?" Chris raised his eyebrows, his tone skeptical.

"Yeah, why not?" Harmony shrugged. "I've had a crush on her since I first grew boobs, basically. And word is she likes the ladies, so why not try to flirt a little and see what happens?"

"If I did that, you'd say I was being creepy," Chris pointed out.

"But I'm not creepy. I'm cute," Harmony countered with a little pout.

"Fair point," Chris laughed. "So, I take it the punch passes inspection?" he asked, pointing to the nearly empty cup in her hand.

"Yes. I, as a scientist, approve this beverage," Harmony said with a sagely nod. "It is sufficiently well-balanced between booziness and sweet yumminess."

"Booziness and yumminess? Are those scientific terms?" Chris asked with a laugh.

"Indeed." Harmony drained the last of her punch. It was good, but the vodka was going straight to her head. *Oh, I feel a little wibbly-wobbly.* It had been a few hours since she'd eaten her sandwich, and if she didn't get something in her stomach before her next drink, she'd be passed-out drunk by seven o'clock.

"I need food," Harmony said.

"Oh dear, wher*ever* could you find food?" Chris said with sweet sarcasm as he gestured at a large consuite table covered with snacks.

"*Real* food, not just chips and candy," Harmony rubbed at her belly. Now that she'd mentioned food, she suddenly realized she was famished.

"We're going to order pizza in just a minute," a guy on the other side of the room called out. "You want in?"

"Yes, please!" Harmony bounded over, introduced herself, and it wasn't long before she had delicious pizza and several new friends: Jeff, Tara, and Jojo. Harmony didn't expect their names would stick, but she tried. They were all nice fannish folks. Chris joined them as well, and they talked about the things that had brought them to JanCon.

Jeff worked in quality assurance for a video game company, and although he was a longtime geek, he was new to the convention scene. Tara had been coming to JanCon on and off for years; she worked at a call center. Jojo was Tara's partner and worked at Starbucks. They were *very* excited about the programming, especially panels with the author guest of honor, somebody Harmony had never heard of—not that she liked to admit that.

I should volunteer in the greenroom with the guests of honor, she thought as they talked. That seemed like the safest way to ensure she'd run into Christina outside of scheduled events. Harmony didn't expect to woo the actress from the other side of an autograph table. She would need one-on-one time. And volunteering in the room—a space set aside for special guests and panelists—seemed like the best way to ensure that. *I love being a volunteer.*

Chapter 2:
Jean

Thursday, 4:23pm

All Jean Lucy Wintz wanted was to get her work done and go home, but interruptions had plagued her all afternoon, and she was nowhere near done. She *needed* to get this bit of code working, or she wouldn't be able to enjoy her long weekend. Unfortunately, her coworkers didn't seem to understand that. Unlike Jean, they weren't anxiety-fueled perfectionists.

Jean took a slow breath before pulling her earbud from her ear. She turned away from her computer screen to look up at her coworker, Hima, who was leaning on the edge of her cube wall, looking at her expectantly.

"Can I help you, Hima?" Jean asked, working to keep the exasperation out of her voice.

"Did you say you'll be out tomorrow or just working from home?" Hima asked.

"Out," Jean nodded curtly. Her irritation was getting increasingly difficult to hide—she'd told the rest of the team about her absence well in advance. Besides which, she only ever worked from home for medical reasons.

"Are you doing anything fun?" Hima wasn't deterred by Jean's cold demeanor. Instead of walking away, as Jean would have preferred, she propped her arms on the top of the cube wall and rested her chin on them. Jean bristled. This move into a casual, conversational stance signified that Hima wanted to chat. *For crying out loud. Why can't she just go away and leave me alone to complete my work?*

"Yes, I'm going to a sci-fi convention," Jean replied curtly.

"Like ComicCon?" Hima asked, her rising inflection signaling to Jean that she knew nothing about conventions. That wasn't a surprise. And it was just as well; the more Hima knew about conventions, the longer the conversation might drag out.

"Yeah, sort of," Jean said. She was being generous—fan-run cons bore little resemblance to the big corporate conventions that occasionally showed up on the news or in mainstream pop culture. Hima continued to stare at her, apparently unsatisfied with Jean's response. "But it's smaller and local," Jean added. "And this is my first time going to this particular convention, so I don't know much more than that. Sorry, I need to get back to this." Jean gestured once more at her computer, which had gone to sleep as they'd talked.

"Oh, okay," Hima backed off. "I'm heading out. Have a nice long weekend. I hope your convention is fun. See you next week."

"Thanks, yeah, see you." Jean popped the earbud back into place and turned once more to her work, hammering out code as fast as her agile fingers would allow. She needed to get this done, and she didn't want to stay all night to do it. She still had to pack.

The details of her pre-convention routine scrolled through the back of her mind as she typed. Jean had a standard and very particular routine for convention planning and preparation. She was self-aware enough to recognize that she didn't *need* to follow the routine— her mild OCD wouldn't stop her from going if she needed to skip a step— but if she did it right, the process would soothe her anxiety. Jean was both nervous and excited for JanCon.

Although she'd been attending conventions since she was born, she hadn't been to a local con since moving to the Chicago area two years ago. Instead she had continued to travel back east to the New England conventions she'd attended as a child. Jean loved the family of fannish folk she had there. She'd grown up at those cons; they were part of who she was. But she hadn't mustered up the courage to step into the local fan-run convention scene in her new home city. That is until she heard about JanCon's special media guest of honor: Christina Darlington.

Jean's excitement at the idea of meeting Christina had overwhelmed her trepidation, and she'd registered for the convention. But that lingering anxiety had crept up on her more and more as the date approached. *It will be fine. It will be great. You'll feel better once you're packed,* she told herself.

When Jean finally finished her work, the office was all but deserted. She pushed her chair under the desk as she donned her coat, pulling her long hair out behind her. She wrapped her rainbow knit scarf around her neck and face as she hastened for the door. Chicago was gray and windy today. It was expected to remain so through the weekend. It was perfect weather for spending time indoors. Although Jean generally considered *any* weather good for staying indoors; she was distinctly *indoorsy.* Sure, Jean enjoyed the occasional walk in the sunshine, but by far her favorite way to spend free time was cuddled up on the sofa with a book or hunched over one of her many ongoing craft projects while a familiar movie or show played in the background.

Jean was an introvert by nature. She appreciated her alone time and was always glad to leave the office behind in favor of her quiet apartment. Jean liked her job —dealing with her coworkers was worth it for the paycheck—but her career didn't define her. Jean may have been a software engineer by profession, but she was a reader, writer, and crafter by any other measure.

When Jean arrived home, she shed her jacket and work attire in favor of roomy sweats. Jean filled a tumbler with ice and pulled out a bottle of Bailey's Irish Cream. The ice cracked as the thick, sweet liqueur filled the glass. Jean swirled her drink. She'd been drinking Bailey's the night she'd first learned that Christina Darlington would be coming to Chicago for JanCon. Jean took a sip, remembering that evening. She had been drinking to numb the pain of her latest heartbreak— drinking and combing the internet for new High School Bites fanfic. She'd searched for anything that would redirect her mind from thoughts of her ex-girlfriend— focusing on stories that centered around the unrequited love between her two favorite characters: Alessia and Francesca.

Their relationship wasn't canon, per se; Alessia had never expressed her love on screen. In the show, their relationship was deep but purely platonic. However, that didn't stop fans like Jean from "shipping" them. Fans like Jean could read between the lines; they saw the romance and felt the unspoken emotions that flowed between Alessia and Francesca. It was clear as day—at least to people like Jean. She was a hopeless romantic. As a teen, she'd read every story she could find that put Alessia and Francesca together. She had written many of her own as well. They were her OTP—her "one true pairing"—and they had consumed her teenage life.

Not only did Jean endlessly ship the two characters, but she had fallen head-over-heels for Alessia, played by the infinitely beautiful Christina Darlington. Despite Jean's proclivity to keep to herself, between the ages of fourteen and eighteen, everybody who met Jean walked away knowing that she *loved* Christina Darlington. It was the one subject on which she could not keep quiet.

Eventually, Jean stopped gushing over the actress and found the courage to start dating and falling in love with actual women. Jean was a serial monogamist; she jumped from one serious relationship to another, each time thinking she'd found "the one" and instead only finding heartbreak. When her relationships crashed and burned, it was Christina to whom she returned. Christina was the one who visited her dreams and awakened her with a gasp; Christina was the one who left Jean breathless and tingling after a night alone in her imagination. Tomorrow imagination would become reality. Tomorrow she would meet Christina in the real world.

Jean shivered at the thought and took a long sip of her Bailey's. *Would I be this nervous if Christina weren't a lesbian?* Jean knew it was ridiculous to fantasize about the possibility of Christina falling in love with her, but she couldn't help herself. Christina was gay, single, and coming here to Chicago. The circumstances were too divinely laid out, too exquisitely conceived not to *try*.

Jean had worked tirelessly to put together the perfect cosplay costumes in preparation for the convention. She wanted to be dressed as the ideal character when she met Christina. That character had to be Francesca.

Despite the lack of overt romance between Francesca and Alessia on the show, Jean and many other High School Bites fans swore they saw genuine affection—even desire—in Alessia's icy blue eyes when she looked at Francesca. When Christina's preference for women had been revealed, it was as if their suspicions had been confirmed. Alessia showed love for Francesca on the screen because Christina was in love with Lindsey MacMillan, the actress who portrayed Francesca—or so the fans believed. And this weekend Jean would *be* Francesca.

Jean set her glass down on one of the many bookshelves lining the walls of her apartment and began her pre-convention routine. She opened her planner and ran her finger down along her meticulously prepared list. She proceeded down the list gathering each item one by one and laying it out or packing it, depending on its use. Extra undergarments, travel-sized toiletries, emergency medications—those all went in the suitcase. Clothing for tomorrow, her toothbrush, and daily meds were all placed where they could be used tonight but not forgotten tomorrow. Then it was time to go over her costumes.

Jean had two different Francesca ensembles she planned to showcase at the convention. Jean laid the first one out on the bed: Francesca's classic daytime look of tiny shorts, a Paddington High t-shirt, and knee-length heeled boots. It didn't seem like much but paired with her dyed-auburn hair, jewelry, fangs, and the right makeup, it was an impressive, if simple, cosplay. Jean made sure each little accessory was accounted for before packing the costume in the suitcase.

Jean slid open her closet door and plucked the second costume down from its hanger. She wanted to try it on and practice her makeup and poses one last time before packing it. This look was much more intense.

For one season, Francesca's style had morphed into something dark and gothic. The character had fallen in with the "wrong crowd." This maleficent period in her life was reflected in her clothing and makeup. Not only was it a more entertaining cosplay to recreate, but it also was one of Jean's favorite story arcs. The storyline culminated in a deeply emotional reunification between Francesca and Alessia that could still bring Jean to tears if she was in the right mood.

Jean slipped on the dress and practiced the makeup routine one last time. Her features were fairly unremarkable—symmetrical but plain, a perfect canvas for transformative make-overs. Jean took her time to carefully apply the layers of makeup. Once complete, Jean stepped back and looked in the mirror. The combination of Francesca's dark makeup and provocative dress was wicked sexy. Jean hoped she could pull it off with a level of confidence befitting the character. She knew she could look the part, but could she live it? She tried out a small, coy smile.

It will be better with the fangs. She could only take the false teeth on and off so many times before they would stop sticking properly. Jean set up her ring light and took pictures of herself in several classic Francesca poses. She flipped through the images. *I have to remember to keep my shoulders back. But this isn't half-bad.* Satisfied, Jean carefully removed the costume and packed it neatly in her suitcase.

Jean picked up her forgotten tumbler. The ice had melted, turning the drink into a blotchy pool of cream and water. She dumped it down the sink and poured herself a fresh glass, which she drank as she moved on to the next step of convention preparation: building her personal schedule.

Although Christina was the catalyst that had prompted Jean to register for JanCon, she wasn't the only reason she was attending. There were other events that she was interested in: panels, parties, and shows. In preparation, she had read several books by Charles Macalester, the author guest of honor. Macalester wrote detailed militaristic science fiction. It wasn't Jean's favorite genre. If given a choice, she preferred fantasy, but she liked plenty of sci-fi and would read just about anything between two covers. After reading Macalester's work she very much looked forward to meeting the author.

Using the convention website, Jean built her own schedule with top priority events, backup options, and time set aside to visit the ongoing parts of the convention, such as the gaming area. She brainstormed possible questions for the guests of honor and other panelists, and gathered bits of information that she might want on-hand for specific panels. Her process may have seemed tedious to other people, but Jean found it relaxing. As she walked through the familiar steps, she could almost forget that this particular convention was new to her. The quirks, traditions, and regular attendees of JanCon might be foreign, but the general concept was the same as any convention. It was a safe place for people who share similar interests to have fun as a community. *And maybe to fall in love.*

Chapter 3:
Harmony

Thursday, 8:10pm

Feeling satisfied that she'd done her share of volunteering for the day, Harmony made her way to the gaming area—a vast, open veranda filled with tables, some empty, some occupied, and one piled high with board games and puzzles. She looked over the pile, taking note of things she might want to play later. She was reading the rules on an unfamiliar but intriguing game—*Talisman*—when somebody covered her eyes from behind.

"Guess who," a husky yet melodic voice whispered in her ear.

Harmony would know that voice anywhere. "Gabby?!" Harmony squealed and turned around to hug her long-time friend. She pulled back to look at Gabby. On the surface Gabby appeared just about the same as ever—scrawny limbs, light brown skin, dark wild hair-—but there was something in her expression that told Harmony everything wasn't as usual.

"What's going on?" Harmony asked, squinting. "I didn't think you were going to make it. I distinctly remember you telling me you wouldn't be here this year."

"Situations change," Gabby said with a wry smile.

"What situations?" Harmony prodded. When Gabby didn't respond, Harmony pressed her again. "Come on, tell me."

"Tam dumped my ass." Gabby's sardonic expression didn't waiver, but Harmony could tell she was hurting on the inside.

"Oh, no! I'm so sorry." Harmony wrapped Gabby in a hug and squeezed.

"Yeah, it sucks. She pretty much broke my heart and ruined my life." Gabby sighed, and Harmony squeezed her harder.

"But hey, at least I that means I can be here," Gabby said, pulling away.

"Well, her loss is my gain. It's great to see you." Harmony smiled brightly at her friend. Gabby needed cheering up, and Harmony knew just the thing. "How's about we get drunk and cuddle? Then, if you want, you can tell me all about it."

"Fantastic idea," Gabby agreed.

The two linked arms and made their way back toward the consuite and bar, where they found a vacant sofa and settled in with drinks. After a few gulps of con punch, Harmony put her arm around Gabby and pulled the thin woman into a warm embrace.

"So, what happened between you and Tammy?" she asked.

Gabby let out a sound that was somewhere between a sigh and a whimper. She snuggled closer to Harmony.

"That bad, huh?" Harmony asked.

Gabby sighed. "I just… I thought this one was forever, you know? Getting dumped always sucks, but this is… really painful." Gabby's voice strained on the last word like she was fighting tears. She swallowed more punch.

"Getting dumped does suck," Harmony said sympathetically, squeezing Gabby's boney shoulder. "What happened?"

"To be honest, I don't fully understand it. *Apparently*, I should have seen it coming," Gabby said, her intonation morphing from sad to bitter. "But I didn't, which just works to prove Tam's point." She sighed.

"What point?" Harmony asked, confused.

"She says I haven't 'grown with the relationship.' According to her, I act like… like because things were good before, they must still be good. Like I assume the relationship will maintain itself without any 'effort' on my part. Or something." Gabby shook her head. "But I didn't change anything. I am who I always have been. And I love her for who she is… But it seems, she can only love me for the person she wants me to grow into."

"That's rough. I'm sorry to hear it. But if it's true that she wants you to change who you are, then it sounds like you're better off without her," Harmony said. "Because you're awesome."

"Thanks. It's just so confusing; I don't understand how she could fall out of love with me so suddenly. It's just… it's a shock. I guess I haven't fully processed it." Gabby tapped her cup on the arm of the sofa. "But I still love her... I think I always will to some degree."

"Even though she's being so awful to you?" Harmony asked.

Gabby lifted one shoulder. "That's how love works, you know."

"I don't really know," Harmony confessed. "I've only ever fallen in love once, so I don't have much experience with… the experience." She snorted. "I'm a love neophyte."

"That surprises me. You date more than anybody I know." Gabby looked sideways at Harmony, her amber-brown eyes narrowed skeptically. "I don't think there's a physicist in the world that gets as much action as you. You're like a nerdy unicorn. You have this wild, pure energy—"

"Oh God, please don't say 'pure energy,'" Harmony interrupted. "I get flashbacks. Far too many people actually think 'pure energy' is a *thing*."

"Is that better or worse than people thinking neutrinos are basically magic?" Gabby lifted an eyebrow with a teasing smirk.

"Those are too ridiculous to even argue with." Harmony rolled her eyes.

"You mean I'm *not* going to get my problem-solving neutrino beam anytime soon?" Gabby cackled.

"Shut up, weren't we talking about my *wild* sex life? Can we go back to that?" Harmony poked Gabby in the side.

"The Others take your *sex life*; I want to know how it's possible that you've only fallen in love once,"

Gabby said. "That seems statistically improbable, given how much you date."

"Love is something that even I, as a scientist, can't seem to suss out with statistics," Harmony said, swirling the punch in her cup as she mulled it over. "Attraction is a simple chemical reaction. It's easy to find somebody visually appealing. So, I date a lot, but I don't fall in love. Generally speaking."

"But you did once?" Gabby asked. "When was that?"

"Her name was Karissa." Harmony thought back. Karissa had seemed *perfect*. She was brilliant, attractive, and she had that *thing*. That *je ne sais quoi*. An undefinable aura caused some switch inside Harmony to flip from like to love. Harmony could never pinpoint exactly what made the difference, what variable distinguished that relationship from all others. She shook her head. "I don't love her anymore. It was so long ago."

"Yeah, I don't think I ever knew her." Gabby squinted at Harmony. "So, you're saying you haven't loved any of your partners since?"

"I've *cared* about them, but there hasn't been that thing, you know? No deep, mad, drive-you-crazy love like I had with Karissa." Harmony regarded her long-time friend. "Why does that surprise you so much?" she asked.

"I guess I always thought I was pickier than you, but I've fallen in love half a dozen times," Gabby said.

"Ah, pickiness has nothing to do with it. I'm *attracted* to more people than you. Like I said, it's a chemical reaction. Evolution or biology has programmed me to look at a lot of people and say, 'oh, yeah, I'd hit that.' But finding somebody attractive— even *extremely* attractive—doesn't mean I'm able to fall in love with them," Harmony explained.

"Come on, you've been closer to your partners than finding them *bangable*," Gabby argued. "You act like you've really liked some of your past partners. Take Chloe, for example—"

"I never loved Chloe, God." Harmony shook her head. She'd stayed with Chloe through some unreasonable behavior, that didn't mean she *loved* her. "She was fun to talk to and have sex with. I liked her, sure. I like a lot of people, but love is different."

"I don't know, Harm, maybe we have different definitions of love. To me, love comes in all shades and degrees." Gabby slowly moved her hand in an arch in front of them, as if painting an imaginary rainbow.

"I'm only talking about romantic love," Harmony clarified.

"Me too—for the most part—but I think the line is blurry," Gabby countered. "I think that's how sometimes friends fall in love over time, and for others, it's like love at first sight. And then, once you're in love, it's not a constant state, apparently. You have to 'grow.'" Gabby snorted and shook her head. "Sometimes you love somebody so much you're willing to lose yourself in them. Or conversely, you can love somebody but not enough to—oh, I don't know—let them go to their favorite sci-fi convention without throwing a fit." Gabby shot Harmony that wry smile again. "Just spit-balling here."

Harmony chuckled. She understood Gabby's take on love at a theoretical level, but for her, the moment she'd fallen in love with Karissa, she'd *known* it. Their connection was instant, electric, and—for a time— unbreakable. When Karissa ended things, Harmony's pain was as fathomless as the sea. That depth of feeling didn't just come around every day. Harmony drank a few more sips of con punch. She didn't like thinking about Karissa. Even though she didn't love her anymore, it was still painful, and it brought up concerns she'd rather ignore. Finding Karissa had been like being struck by lightning. Could lightning strike twice? The fear that Karissa had been her "one true love" was cliché and illogical, but Harmony wrestled with it in the back of her mind, nonetheless

"Maybe we do define love differently, but I only know how to operate based on my own definitions," Harmony mused. "I'm not sure about the idea of friends 'falling in love over time.' Take us for example. You're attractive; I'd totally make out with you. But I don't think I'm likely to ever fall in love with you. If I were, it would have happened by now."

"That's so funny because totally I love you, but I don't want to make out, thanks," Gabby replied with a laugh.

"Your loss," Harmony teased. "I'm told I'm quite good at it." Harmony stood up and stretched; her head was already swimming with the effects of alcohol, but it was a pleasant feeling.

"You don't have to run away; I like the cuddles," Gabby protested.

"I'm not leaving; I'm just out of booze. Want me to grab you another drink?" Harmony asked, shaking her empty cup. Gabby nodded and handed over her own plastic receptacle. Harmony walked back to the bar and helped herself to another few ladles worth of fully-leaded con punch.

The guy running the bar barely looked up. He was familiar. *Tom or Chad or something?* He didn't seem to mind that she was serving herself; he must have recognized her as well. The casual familiarity was one thing that made this Harmony's favorite con. She felt like part of the family here, and as with a large extended family, although she might not always remember the names of each distant relative, they were still part of the same tree.

"Hey, so, I have a question then," Gabby began when Harmony returned to the sofa.

"And I might have an answer," Harmony said, settling back down into Gabby's embrace.

"Do you *want* to fall in love?" Gabby asked.

"Oh, yes, absolutely I do." Harmony was surprised by the question. *Doesn't everybody want to fall in love? Well, not aromantics, I suppose. But she can't think that I'm aro.*

"Well, then why do you hook up with people you know you won't fall in love with?" Gabby tilted her head and looked at Harmony questioningly.

Harmony wagged her head back and forth, noting the soft slushy sensation of drunkenness. "I have sex with people because I enjoy it. I don't see the point in being a monk until I find love. There are way too many cute girls out there for that."

"Just girls?" Gabby asked, one eyebrow raised.

"I've been riding the gay side of my bi-cycle lately." Harmony replied with a shrug. It was true; when she closed her eyes and dreamed of sex, it was beautiful breasts, smooth legs, and curving hips that filled her mind. Harmony hadn't had sex in quite a while, longer than she would like to admit. She was an accomplished masturbater, if there were awards for such things, she would be well decorated. But her imagination--coupled with help from the internet--could only sustain her for so long. She was *really* ready to get laid this weekend. *Oh, Ms. Darlington, could you be the one to break the dry spell?* Visions of Christina's body pressed against her own floated through Harmony's inebriated mind.

"Earth to Harmony." Gabby poked at her side.

"Huh?"

"Where'd you go? You totally spaced out there for a while." Gabby had a glint in her eye that told Harmony that she wasn't without theories.

"Just daydreaming about Christina Darlington again," Harmony admitted; there didn't seem to be a point in denying it.

"Well, good luck with that." Gabby sat back and sighed. "Ahh, it's nice to be back here."

"Glad to have you," said Harmony. "This weekend has the potential to be *epic*."

Friday, 10:00am

Harmony woke up bright and early Friday morning — or at least early for a con morning. She was out of her room by ten a.m., dressed in jeans, Hufflepuff socks, and a JanCon t-shirt. She walked briskly across the hotel in search of breakfast. Considering how late she'd been up the night before, her energy level was surprisingly high. But she still needed her morning fuel-up. The consuite was busy, so Harmony made her way down the hall to the greenroom. She poured herself a cup of coffee with cream and sugar and gave the food offerings a once-over. *Ah, lemon bars, the food of my people.* As Harmony helped herself to food, she chatted briefly with

Candice, the woman running the greenroom. Harmony had a passing familiarity with her but wouldn't have called her a friend.

"Nice spread," Harmony said, gesturing to the food. "I'm so glad I volunteer."

"You can't be in here just because you're a volunteer; you need to be a panelist or on con-com."

"Con-com?"

"The convention committee..." Candice said, eyeing Harmony with sudden suspicion.

"Oh, duh." Harmony slapped her forehead. "I knew that. I guess I'm not as awake as I thought. I suppose I really need this coffee, huh?" Harmony smiled, but Candice still looked skeptical. "I should amend my prior statement," Harmony said. "I'm so glad I'm on a panel."

"Which panel?"

"Ask a scientist," Harmony said through a mouthful of lemon bar. "What about you? Are you on a panel?"

"No, I don't like public speaking. I'm on con-com," Candice responded, her demeanor relaxing into friendly companionability. "I'm the guest of honor coordinator."

"Oh! Really?" Harmony perked up. "As such, do you happen to know when Christina Darlington will be arriving?" she asked hopefully.

"Should be any minute," Candice replied, glancing at her phone. "The itinerary said she'd be arriving in the late morning."

"Oh! That's great!" Harmony shoved the rest of the lemon bar in her mouth. "I'm so excited to meet her."

"Well, if you want to welcome her and point her this way, I have her packet," Candice said, pointing a thumb toward the filing box on the floor next to her chair.

"I could take it to her," Harmony offered, bouncing on her toes eagerly.

"I'd prefer she come pick it up," Candice said, shaking her head. "That's what she's been told already. So, you don't need to go down to welcome her—"

"Oh, but I want to!" Harmony grinned. "See you later!" She bounced out of the greenroom, down the hall toward the front of the hotel.

Harmony rounded the corner and immediately caught sight of Christina Darlington, standing on the opposite side of the lobby. Harmony's insides went to jelly. Christina was as beautiful in person as she was on TV. Her long blonde hair cascaded over her shoulders in soft waves. The skinny jeans she wore clung tightly to her slender body and highlighted every curve from her calves all the way up to her perky little behind.

"It's nice to meet you," she said with an easy smile that made Harmony's skin tingle with delight. Harmony let her fingers linger, lightly brushing against Christina's palm as she withdrew from their handshake. She caught Christina's eye and held it. *I'm flirting with you*, she thought, willing her to understand. It might have been wishful thinking, but she thought she saw a look of recognition cross Christina's face. Harmony felt her smile widen.

"I'm serious; if there's anything you need, please let me know," she said.

"Thank you, that's very sweet. I'm going to go get settled in my room first, but then I'll go pick up that packet. Maybe I'll see you there, *Harmony*."

The sound of her name on Christina's lips nearly knocked her off her feet. "Yeah, awesome, cool..." Harmony backed off slightly to make it clear that she wasn't just some crazy stalker fan. *Just act normal. Or as normal as you're able.* "I'll be in and out of the greenroom all day, so I guess I'll see you around!" She gave Christina a quick wave and, with considerable effort, turned her back and walked away from the love of her adolescent life.

Was that too much? I probably shouldn't have said, "I'm a big fan." *That was dumb. She probably thinks I'm loony.* Harmony risked a glance back; Christina was waiting by the elevator. She caught Harmony's eye, and Harmony felt blood rush to her face. *I look like such a fangirl; there's no way I have a chance.* Christina flashed her a small, secretive smile, and Harmony's heart began to sing. She smiled back. *But maybe I do. Stranger things have happened.*

Chapter 4:
Jean

Jean woke up with anxious, excited energy pumping through her veins, making her head light and her heart race. She took her meds, brushed her teeth, and put the last items into her suitcase—the final pieces of the pre-con routine. Jean cross-checked her packing list one last time to ensure she hadn't forgotten anything. She triple-checked the items she was most concerned about: her costumes, medications, and phone charger. It was all packed neatly in place. Jean took a deep breath. *It's going to be fine—better than fine. It's going to be fun.*

Jean closed the suitcase and zipped it shut, sliding it off the bed and onto the carpet with a soft *thud*. Jean reached for her messenger bag, pillow, and stuffed bear. Slinging the bag across her back, she tucked the other two items under her arm, pulled up the suitcase handle, and rolled it out of her room.

Jean double-checked that the door to her apartment was locked before rolling her suitcase down to the lobby and calling a Lyft. She hated using a driving service; getting in a stranger's car always set her nerves on end, and the distance to the convention hotel was so short it felt foolish to drive at all. Nevertheless, the thought of wheeling her suitcase through the city—pillow and bear in her arms—made her nauseous with anxiety. She just couldn't do it. And although it made her anxious, a Lyft would be significantly cheaper than taking her own car and parking in the hotel garage. So as much as she hated being driven, she couldn't justify any other option.

Luckily, her Lyft driver was one of the shut-up-and-drive types, and Jean arrived at the hotel without incident. She tipped generously and left the driver a glowing review before pulling open the door and stepping into the hotel.

Once inside, Jean could feel her anxiety tick down a notch. The open lobby was moderately crowded with people of all ages, some in costume, others sporting t-shirts with geeky references printed across the front, "Prune Juice: A Warrior's Drink" and "Mordor Fun Run: One does not simply walk." Jean smiled. She knew this crowd; she might not know these specific individuals, but they reminded her of her family and friends back home, and that put Jean at ease.

None of the people who walked by looked at her twice. *I probably don't look like I'm here for the convention.* She needed to get her badge and get up to her room to change. Jean was very aware of her "mundane" appearance—she could blend in wherever she went, which sometimes made her feel like she didn't fully fit in anywhere. Nobody looking at her would say, "oh, that's one of my people." Except for when she was in costume. Until then, she may have seen them as family, but they didn't see her at all.

Jean checked in and was waiting for the elevator when she saw her—Christina Darlington—standing across the lobby, barely ten yards away. Jean lost all feeling in her limbs and face as she observed Christina casually *exist* in real life, in the same room, breathing the same air. *Don't forget to breathe*, Jean reminded herself.

Christina was *stunning*. She was just as Jean had always imagined, if slightly shorter. She had hardly aged at all. Her hair looked so smooth, the blonde so natural—although Jean knew it wasn't. Jean touched her own auburn hair and wished she'd spent the money to have it professionally colored. She watched Christina gesture with her delicate, perfectly manicured fingers.

Jean wanted to take her hand and entwine those fingers with her own, to feel those polished nails scrape down her back. Jean shivered. *You're getting ahead of yourself, Jean. There are a lot of people interested in Christina who she'd be more likely to notice. People who might have the courage to actually approach her rather than stare at her like a stupefied muggle.*

As if to prove her point, a buxom young woman with strawberry curls and a broad smile bounded up to Christina and began to chat with her as if they were long-lost friends. Jean immediately knew the woman was a fan—not just because the convention t-shirt she was wearing stretched thin over her ample breasts, but because of her bubbly, open energy that said she knew who she was, knew she was a little odd, and didn't care.

The woman had a bright rainbow "Queer Fan" ribbon affixed to her badge. She was openly gay and blatantly flirting. Jean couldn't compete with that level of bold self-assurance—not in her current "mundane" state anyway. Jean's chest burned with envy as she watched the two talk. *Why can't that be me?*

As much as she yearned to talk to the actress, when Christina began to move in Jean's direction, Jean panicked and fled. She rushed into an elevator and jammed the "door close" button with her thumb. She had to get out of there before she could ruin Christina's first impression of her by being so very forgettable.

Jean's heart thundered in her ears as she made her way up to her room. She hated that she'd just avoided meeting the one person in the world she'd wanted to meet more than anybody else, but she just hadn't been ready yet. *I need my costume,* she told herself. *But what if that isn't enough? What if I never find the courage?* She was breathing heavily and shaking all over when she reached her room. *I am having a panic attack.* She stripped off her clothes and burrowed beneath the soft hotel comforter. *Calm down, Jean.* Her heart hammered against her ribcage as she lay curled in bed, wearing nothing but her panties. *You will be brave enough when you are Francesca.* Jean closed her eyes and willed her nerves to relax, but they stubbornly refused. The anxiety made her chest tight and her breathing painful.

Jean knew a few ways to calm a mild panic attack, but she didn't want to take her "as needed" medication. Instead, she slipped one hand inside the waistband of her black cotton panties. *Be Francesca; find Alessia.* She slid her fingers down until they found her clit. She sighed as she began to touch herself—softly at first, her mind focused on fantasy.

"I want you, Francesca." Alessia stood before her, stunning in her black gown, her hair down around her shoulders. There was emotion in her crystal blue eyes. But was it genuine desire?

"Do you? Do you really?" Francesca circled Alessia once, slowly, like a tiger circling prey. Do you really want me?" she repeated, her tone dark and almost threatening.

"Yes," Alessia whispered, and Francesca stopped before her.

"Show me," she commanded, and Alessia did. She kissed Francesca, grabbing her ass, and pulling her in with firm assurance. Francesca slipped the strap from Alessia's shoulder, peeling her dress down to reveal Alessia's breast and her hard, peach-pink nipple. Francesca hesitated, but Alessia took her hand and guided it into place over her bare chest.

"You show me," she whispered in Francesca's ear. Francesca squeezed the soft, warm flesh.

Lying in bed, eyes still closed, Jean touched her own breast, rolling her nipple between her thumb and forefinger.

Alessia guided Francesca's other hand between her legs. Francesca eagerly complied, inching her fingers deeper between Alessia's thighs until Alessia moaned.

"Yes, touch me."

Jean mimicked her imagination, rubbing her clit, squeezing her breast harder and faster, moaning as she did. *"Touch me."*

In her mind, the scenery of High School Bites faded away, replaced by her own bedroom. Jean was herself, and it was Christina whom she touched and who touched her. *Oh God, Christina.* Christina pushed Jean down onto the bed, lowering her head between her legs. *Oh God, Christina.* She could see Christina's blonde head bounded by her own pale thighs; she could feel Christina's tongue on her clit. *Slow down. Oh God, I'm going to cum.*

Jean wasn't ready for her fantasy to be over, but she couldn't stop herself—the orgasm overwhelmed her, and she cried out as her hips lifted off the bed. She collapsed back down with a groan and a whimper. *If imagining her is this good, how amazing would the real thing be?* Jean lay still as her racing heart slowed to a steady normal rhythm. She took a deep breath, her anxiety dissipating along with the orgasm.

Jean lifted herself off the bed before she could risk falling asleep. She hopped into the shower, rinsed off her slick juices, and shaved her legs. The shorts of her costume were *quite* short, and she wanted her legs to look as good as possible. Once she was clean and dried, Jean set her makeup on the counter next to reference images of Francesca and got to work. Jean bore a close enough resemblance to Francesca such that with the right makeup, the likeness became uncanny. Jean didn't wear much makeup in day-to-day life, but cosplay makeup was an art form to her, and she'd perfected the skills needed to transform her face from plain-Jane-pretty to striking, head-turning beauty.

Makeup done to her satisfaction, Jean squeezed into the tiny Paddington High t-shirt she'd screen-printed herself and a pair of store-bought short-shorts. Jean had made Francesca's signature choker and bracelet by hand because there was no way to purchase exact replicas. She was very proud of them; the costume's little details were what took it from pretty good to perfect.

Jean secured the tiny false fangs to her top canine teeth. The teeth were the least comfortable part of the costume, but they helped her get into character more than any other element. She could forget what she looked like—could ignore her skimpy clothing—but the acute and mildly painful pressure of the sharp little teeth was a constant reminder. When she was wearing them She wasn't Jean, the introverted bookworm. She was Francesca, the sexy, confident, ass-kicking vampire.

When the teeth were securely in place, Jean zipped up her high-heeled boots and stood in front of the hotel room's full-length mirror. *Why hello there, Francesca.* She smirked and Francesca smirked back at her, one white fang poking out between her darkly painted lips. *Let's go find, Alessia, shall we?*

Chapter 5:
Harmony

Friday, 11:14am

Harmony looked at her watch; her next volunteer shift wasn't until the afternoon. She had signed up to manage the greenroom and set up one of the ballrooms for Christina's panel. But there were hours until then. She pulled her pocket program from her back pocket and flipped to the Friday schedule. *The dealer's room is open; I could go check that out.* Harmony enjoyed meandering through the massive convention space, packed with booths and tables selling various wares—from comics to costumes and everything in-between. Harmony would sometimes pick up a book or t-shirt, but she wasn't a big spender. As a physics post-doc, she wasn't exactly flush with cash, but she loved a little geeky window-shopping.

Harmony strolled casually past the different tables, stopping now and then to examine an item more closely. She stopped at a booth selling buttons, bumper stickers, and decals. She briefly considered a *Serenity* decal before deciding her car was over-stickered as it.

She moved on down the row. One corner of the room was taken over by an expansive costume shop. Corsets, skirts, and kilts hung on a tall display rack. Harmony's eyes were drawn to the corsets. Rigid boning covered enticingly with fabric or leather—they came in dozens of colors and styles. She *loved* the look of women in corsets. They were common attire at the convention, and Harmony appreciated that. She brushed her fingers over her favorite one. It was made all in black, with a subtle Victorian floral pattern, smooth silk piping, and ruffles across the bustline. Harmony traced the curve of the steel boning beneath the sleek fabric. *This is sexy as hell.*

"Can I help you with anything?" A petite middle-aged woman with a measuring tape around her neck approached Harmony.

"Oh no, sorry, just looking." Harmony began to back away.

"You sure? You'd look great in that one," the woman said. Harmony shook her head. As much as she loved the look on other women, she had never worn one herself. It would make her far too self-conscious.

Harmony's con attire consisted of geeky t-shirts, hoodies, jeans, and sometimes pajama pants. Not cleavage-boosting bodices; Harmony had far too much cleavage for that, in her opinion.

"No, thank you," Harmony gave the woman an awkward smile, turned away, and strolled toward the large sword display a couple of tables down. She picked up a small sword, enjoying the weight of it in her hand. *If I did wear costumes, then I'd have an excuse to get a sword.* She glanced at the price tag. *Three-hundred bucks?!* She set it down. That was more than a month of groceries. She shook her head and wandered off toward the closest used book sales table. Books she could afford. Books always fit. *Can't go wrong with books.*

Harmony chatted amicably with the bookseller as she dug through the bin of used books. After settling on a beat-up old copy of Protector by Larry Niven, Harmony checked her watch. Christina would be speaking on a panel that afternoon about the romantic allure of vampires. It was called something like: *Why are Vampires so Hot?* Harmony didn't care so much about the subject of the panel; High School Bites was the only vampire-based fandom she'd ever gotten into. In general, she preferred science fiction, especially that of the Star Trek and Ender's Game variety, but she wanted to listen to Christina speak and have the chance to talk to her again.

After paying for her book, Harmony had just enough time to swing by her room. She dropped off her purchase and riffled through her duffle for the pack of candy that she had brought for Christina. *It's the little things, right?* Candy in hand, Harmony made her way back down the elevator to the panel.

Christina was already there when Harmony arrived. She stood next to the dais, chatting with a woman in the most impeccable *Francesca* cosplay Harmony had ever seen. The remarkable likeness momentarily stopped Harmony in her tracks.

Francesca—or the woman dressed like her—was tall and lean with delicate model-like features. Her soft curves were made readily apparent by the costume's skimpy nature. The teeny-tiny Paddington Academy t-shirt stretched tight over the woman's small round breasts and was short enough to show off a few inches of her smooth, flat abdomen. Her long, shapely legs perfectly suited Francesca's signature short-shorts and tall boots. Even her jewelry was impeccable. The woman's hair was a flat auburn color rather than the deep red of the character, but aside from that, it was a spot-on likeness. She looked perfect alongside Christina.

I hope to God this woman's not gay. At any other time, Harmony would have prayed for such a beautiful woman to be gay, but not today. Today she was a potential rival. If this woman liked Christina the way Harmony did, Harmony would have her work cut out for her, and she feared she wouldn't fare well in competition with the gorgeous cosplayer. Harmony quickly pushed away the thought and bounded over to the two.

"Can I get a picture of your costume?" she asked. The woman nodded, and Christina started to step out of frame, but Harmony waved her back in. "No, no, I want you two together. The cosplay is so good you really look like Francesca and Alessia, reunited. If only your clothes matched, it would be like being on set."

"Well, you won't catch me in those tiny shorts again," Christina laughed. "You must be freezing, sweety." She put an arm around the woman, who was blushing deeply. Harmony felt a pinprick of jealousy, seeing this woman receive such close attention from

Christina. She snapped a few pictures before pocketing her phone and thrusting out her hand.

"I'm sorry I didn't get your name. I'm Harmony, by the way," Harmony said as she shook the cosplayer's hand.

"Jean," she answered simply. Christina touched Jean lightly on the shoulder.

"Well, Jean, it was so wonderful to meet you. I should be going," Christina nodded her head in the direction of the panel stage. "But maybe we can meet up again."

"Yeah, and I can take a modern-day Francesca and Alessia photo," Harmony chimed in. "You know when you're both wearing *pants* like *adults*."

Both women ignored Harmony's joke, which was just as well; it had come out sounding more sarcastic than she had intended. Harmony watched as Christina lightly brushed Jean's arm before moving away toward the dais. *Is Christina hitting on Jean?* It sure seemed like it to Harmony, and she wasn't particularly pleased with the notion. The pinprick of jealousy grew a bit sharper.

"I brought you a bottle of water and some candy," Harmony said, following Christina to her chair and holding out her offerings.

"Thank you, I appreciate that… Oh, sour gummies are my absolute favorite. How did you know?" Christina beamed. Harmony merely shrugged. She didn't need to tell the actress that her fans knew just about everything there was to know about her. That sounded a little too stalker-ish.

"I guess we have similar tastes, although I only like the red and green ones personally, the others… I mean, come on, lemon?" Harmony stuck out her tongue and made a sour face.

Christina laughed her sweet melodious laugh. "I like lemon just fine, but it seems we might have some other tastes in common," Christina said coyly, nodding at the Queer Fan ribbon Harmony wore. Harmony ran a finger over the shimmery rainbow ribbon.

"Ah, yes, I believe we do." Harmony looked at Christina and grinned. "So, I guess in this instance I *am* the 'snack' from the greenroom."

Christina laughed again, and Harmony felt warm all over. She knew she was blushing, knew her joke had been corny as hell, but she didn't care. It felt *wonderful* to be interacting with this incredible woman in real life. Harmony's face almost hurt from smiling as she helped Christina settle in her place on the dais.

"If there's anything else you need, *anything at all,* just let me know," Harmony reminded Christina again. Christina nodded, and Harmony excused herself to join the audience.

Harmony settled into a seat in the front row, and the panel got underway. Each panelist spoke briefly about their experience with the subject before starting a general discussion. In addition to Christina, there were two authors, a film professor, and a moderator. The moderator didn't seem to have any qualifications beyond being 'totally *obsessed* with everything vampire,' but he did a good job keeping the conversation flowing. It was entertaining, even without having deep knowledge of the genre.

The beautiful cosplayer—Harmony had already forgotten her name—asked one of the first questions during the "Q&A" portion of the panel. She stood while she spoke; her voice was simultaneously soft and perfectly clear from the other side of the room. She had a very faint accent; her A-sounds and dropped Rs made Harmony suspect she might be from the east coast. Harmony was no linguist, but she enjoyed analyzing accents. The woman's question was well thought out and articulated, and Christina seemed to take particular delight in answering.

Harmony shifted awkwardly in her seat. The woman of her dreams was smiling at this stranger like they were the only people in the room. Harmony tried not to be envious of the apparent connection between these two women, but she couldn't help it. *Cosplay lady is probably just fangirling. She doesn't seem like she'd be into women. It's not worth being jealous. Christina was friendly to me too.* Harmony looked at the woman, sitting tall and listening to Christina with calm, focused attention. She was all poise and beauty. For some reason, it made Harmony's chest uncomfortably tight. *She's the most attractive fan at the convention, and she knows it.*

When Christina finished answering, Harmony felt her hand shoot up. She didn't really have a good question, but she wanted to say *something*—or at least look like she had something worth saying.

Christina made eye contact with her and raised an eyebrow. "Yes? Harmony, right?"

"Yeah, uh, I…" Harmony stammered, trying to think of something on the spot. *Come on, think…* "Did the fake blood taste bad?" Harmony blurted out the second it occurred to her. "I mean, when you played Alessia, you were always licking your fingers; I wondered what that tasted like." *I wonder what you taste like*, Harmony thought.

"The blood was mostly corn syrup and food coloring," Christina replied. "We used it so much, and since we often worked through lunch, I used to joke that I really was living off the stuff." Christina laughed at the memory. Harmony grinned at her. Christina's laugh was delightful; Harmony could sit and listen to it all day long.

"Please keep questions to the topic of this panel," the moderator cut in. "If you have general questions for Ms. Darlington, you can go to her solo Q and A panel later this afternoon."

"Oh, I'll be there," Harmony said and gave Christina an exaggerated wink, prompting another smile from her. The moderator looked at Harmony with a pursed, irritated expression. *Oh, whatever.* She knew she should have saved that question for the appropriate time, but she wasn't going to lose any sleep over it. She'd gotten Christina to laugh, and that was all that mattered.

Chapter 6:
Jean

Friday, 1:30pm

After the panel wrapped up, fans immediately swarmed the dais—each hoping for a personal word with Christina and the other panelists. Jean stood and made for the door. She was pleased with the conversation she'd had with Christina before, and she didn't care to contend with other fans for her attention now. However, there was one thing that put a damper on the moment: Harmony. There was something about that bubbly, curly-haired woman that made Jean's stomach clench uneasily.

Let it go, Jean, she told herself. *Christina answered your question: you got her attention.* Her first interaction with Christina had gone better than she'd initially expected. *I know I can talk to her. Shouldn't that help my anxiety?*

When Jean emerged from the room, she turned toward the dealer's gally. She had some time before the next event she planned to attend, and she always loved perusing the goods at conventions.

On the way to the dealer's room, Jean was stopped several times by convention-goers who wanted pictures of her costume. Jean happily obliged, striking her practiced poses. Only one of the people who asked for a photo was a little skeevy, giving off the impression that he wanted a photo of her because he thought she looked hot rather than because she'd reproduced Francesca's look so well. The rest were kind, genuine fans.

"Would you mind taking a selfie with me where it looks like you're going to bite me?" one nervous young man asked in a cracking voice. It wasn't exactly an easy pose to strike, but she agreed, and after a few awkward attempts, they managed to take a picture that looked pretty good.

"Can I get your number?" he asked after. "You know, so I can send you the picture," he added hastily.

"How about my email instead?" Jean offered, and the man nodded.

"Sure, here; go ahead and type it in." He handed her his phone. "My name's Tim."

"Nice to meet you, Tim," Jean said, handing back the phone. "I'm Jean."

"Would you maybe be interested in getting together some time?" Tim asked, smiling nervously, his voice rising uncertainly. Jean could tell it had taken him a great deal of courage to ask.

"I don't think so, sorry. I'm a lesbian... and not very social," Jean said honestly.

Tim's smile wavered but didn't fall. "Oh, okay. See you around. Great costume."

Jean thanked him and continued on her way to the dealer's room. For some reason, the interaction with awkward-but-polite Tim had a calming effect on Jean's nerves. The crowds there, with their mix of friendly and awkward, were soothing to her. She wished she'd had the courage to attend the con immediately after moving to the area. Of course, Christina wouldn't have been there, but it would have been nice to conncct with people in her new home. Although she wasn't a very social person—an introvert by any definition—she wasn't a total recluse. Having friends nearby would make Illinois feel more like home, even if she only saw them a few times a year.

The dealer's gally was larger than Jean had expected. She strolled through the maze of tables and displays, carefully looking everything over but never stopping her slow, methodic progress. Jean had a process when it came to shopping at a convention. Once she had completed one appraising circuit of the room, she went back to the beginning and retraced her path, this time stopping to thoroughly inspect anything that had caught her eye on the first go-round.

Jean stopped at three shops on her second pass. At the first, she bought an adorable little ceramic Pocket Dragon figurine. She delighted in acquiring small figurines and trinkets and placing them among the books on her many bookshelves. She took care to put each little thing in an intentional, meaningful location. She paired items and books like a sommelier picking the perfect wine to go with a meal.

The dragon was the easiest purchasing decision of the day—although Jean didn't yet know precisely where it would live amongst her books. It wasn't overly expensive, and it was just so cute. The rest would take much more consideration. *Remember, you don't have to buy today, you don't have to get anything else at all, you already got the dragon,* Jean told herself as she stepped up to the sizable costuming shop. Although Jean preferred to make all her cosplay pieces, certain things were worth purchasing—things like corsets.

Jean took her time looking at each item, from steampunk goggles and bondage collars to the large, multi-layer skirts and full-length leather trench coats. Jean ran her fingers along the hem of a velvet cloak; it wasn't nearly as well-made as the one sitting at home in her closet, the one she had sewn herself.

"Can I help you find anything?" A woman wearing a tape measure about her neck appeared just behind Jean's right shoulder. Jean jumped slightly, shying away from the close-talking woman.

"Oh, no, just looking," Jean said quickly. The woman was older with knobby knuckles and a stance that said she'd already been on her feet for a long time today. Jean suspected she was the owner of the shop.

"Okay, let me know if I can answer any questions," the woman said, backing off slightly but never turning away from Jean.

Jean returned her attention to the displays, careful to keep her expression neutral as she inspected each item, checking quality and price. She could feel the eyes of the proprietor on her; it made it hard to concentrate on the costumes. Jean had been interested in the corsets. On her first lap, a smooth black one had caught her eye. It was the only corset of its kind in the shop; all the others were two-toned. Jean was drawn to the elegant balance of simplicity and detail. She wanted to inspect it more closely, but she was too uncomfortable under the woman's gaze to do more than take a quick peek at the size. *It would fit, but the lady would want me to try it on.* Jean glanced back; the woman smiled at her, and Jean hurriedly moved away from the corset, feigning disinterest. The moment the woman looked away, Jean fled the shop altogether.

You're being ridiculous. You know you would have to talk to an employee if you bought anything. Why can't you just interact with them while you shop? Jean didn't have an answer for herself; she only knew that if she wanted the corset, she would have to come back later when her anxiety was lower. *What if it's not there when I come back?* Jean shook her head and straightened her back. *Then I won't get it, it's fine. Be Francesca. Francesca wouldn't give a shit.* But Jean had a hard time staying in character amidst the chaos in the dealer's room. She gave the bookshop a longing look. The books, lined up neatly across tables and shelves, called to her. But a man was sitting at the booth, waiting. He had no other customers. *If I go over there, he's going to talk to me*. She hurried past the books and out of the room.

Jean stood in the vast open veranda, rolling her shoulders and trying to get back into a confident Francesca mindset. She ran her tongue over the pointy little vampire fangs. *Come on, Francesca. Where are you?* Unfortunately, Jean still felt like herself—the tingling discomfort of anxiety continued to irritate her lungs. *I need to reset.* She didn't want to go back to her room, so instead, she sought out a bathroom.

Hesitantly she stepped in front of the washroom mirror and let out a breath of relief. The face that stared back at her was not plain, anxious Jean; it was fierce, beautiful, *confident* Francesca. She bent and flipped her hair forward, then back; it fell into place, framing her face with soft waves. Jean pulled back her shoulders and pushed out her chest. Out of the corner of her eye, she could see other women looking at her with a mixture of awe and contempt. *Bite me*, Francesca said inside of Jean's mind, and Jean smirked. *There you are, Francesca.* She looked herself over once more before sauntering out of the ladies room.

Jean maintained her poise and confidence throughout the afternoon as she attended panels. Her favorite was titled *Fanfic is Real Writing* and included several real published authors admitting that they too wrote fan fiction—sometimes even of their own works. Jean left the panel lighthearted and inspired. Thoughts of her own fanfic floated through her mind as she sashayed across the hotel in true Francesca style.

Jean ate alone at the edge of the consuite—her mind half in the world of High School Bites, half in this special corner of the real world, surrounded by people who were like her. Fans who understood the desire to be entirely immersed in another universe—someplace filled with magic, splendor, and wicked hot vampires.

Jean felt like a wicked hot vampire, and she bathed in that sensation. She sat up straight in her seat, careful to keep her bare midriff flat, as Francesca would. She ate slowly, wrapping her dark red lips carefully around each bite to keep her lipstick on her and not her food. Jean knew it probably looked a bit sensual, but that too was in character for Francesca.

Francesca was sensual, sexy, and a little slutty. In the show, she seduced scores of young men with her vampiric allure. In Jean's imagination—and in the stories she'd written—Francesca turned that magnetic sexual energy on Alessia. Jean imagined herself as

Francesca, slowly pulling Alessia in, stroking her cheek, kissing her neck, nipping at her with her sharp little fangs—making Alessia gasp before pressing their lips together in a series of deep, hungry kisses. Jean sighed to herself, consumed by the daydream as she chewed her dinner.

"I've never seen anybody make potato salad look so… scrumptious." A man's voice snapped Jean back into reality. She blinked. While she'd been lost in thought, a guy had seated himself next to her. He was about her age with short dark hair, a round face, and close-set eyes. He was sitting there, cup-a-soup in hand, watching her.

"Oh, I, yeah, it's okay," she stammered. Thrown off by his sudden, intense attention, Jean felt the edges of her Francesca confidence begin to fray. She sat up taller, trying to regain her poise. "Eating with lipstick can be a bit tricky," she said. "I don't normally wear lipstick."

"You should, it's really hot," the man said bluntly, and Jean felt her cheeks warm. *How would Francesca react?*

"Thank you," Jean responded with a slight nod of her head. She turned her attention back to her food, but the man persisted.

"So, do you like vampires exclusively, or are you into the whole supernatural genre?" he asked. Jean turned to face him once more. His badge said Jeff, and his expression said, "I'm going to talk to you whether you like it or not."

"Oh, I like it all. Although I'd say fantasy is my favorite genre, I'll read just about anything—"

"Have you read the Wheel of Time series?" Jeff asked before Jean could even take a breath. "Not just watched the show," he added with a scoff.

She assured him that she had indeed read the books. She expected a diatribe about the show, but Jeff quickly explained that he had met Brandon Sanderson on *several* occasions. *He just wants to brag.* Jeff grew agitated when Jean didn't immediately fall over herself to sound interested in his experience with the famous author. He proceeded to quiz her on ridiculously small plot points and details of Sanderson's books as if he didn't believe she'd been telling the truth. Jean felt her poise once more start to unravel and knew she needed to get out of there. She made a show of looking at her phone, pretending it had vibrated.

"Oh, I'm sorry, I have to go," she said, standing abruptly.

"Okay, we can talk more about it later," Jeff said with no indication that he understood that Jean was simply trying to get away from him. Jean nodded absently as she hurried off, striding purposefully in no particular direction.

Once she was safely out of sight of Jeff, Jean took a moment to note the time and check her schedule. Christina Darlington's solo question and answer session would start in fifteen minutes. Jean decided to go to the panel room early; she could easily kill fifteen minutes on her phone. *Maybe I could write out some of the Francesca/Alessia scenes I came up with at the last panel.*

Jean took the long way around the hotel, hoping to avoid Jeff. She didn't think he meant any offense when he'd basically asked to check her geek credentials—he was clearly a socially awkward guy—but she didn't feel like spending time with people who reminded her that their base perception of her was "hot girl" and not "fellow geek." There were more pleasant people to be around. *Like Christina.*

Maybe if I'm early, and she's early, we can talk again, Jean thought hopefully as she opened the door to the convention room. It was the correct room; there was a single name card on stage, and it read *Christina Darlington*, but the place was empty. Jean rechecked the time. *Thirteen minutes.* She picked a seat on the end of the middle row, sat down, and began to type on her phone.

As people trickled in, Jean continued to glance up from her phone, hoping that one of the faces she saw would be Christina's. As she did, she caught sight of a few somewhat familiar faces—people she'd seen at other panels—including the loud, bouncy, buxom Harmony. She caught Harmony's eye, and the woman scowled. *What did I do to her?* Before Jean could react, Jeff walked through the door, and Jean quickly averted her gaze. *Don't sit by me, don't sit by me,* she thought. Jean watched from the corner of her vision as Jeff looked her over, turned, and sat beside Harmony.

Jean was glad he hadn't sat beside her. Nonetheless, when he so pointedly picked Harmony over her, Jean felt her once bright sense of belonging dim further. She wasn't jealous that annoying Jeff had chosen to sit by somebody else, but at the same time, she felt envious of Harmony. She had natural charisma—in that bubbly fannish way—that drew people toward her. All of Jean's "charisma" was put on when she donned her costume.

Don't think about it. Be Francesca. Be present. Jean held on to her put-on poise through the panel. It was easy to feel good when Christina was speaking. Christina had been running a couple minutes behind, so nobody had the chance to talk to her before the panel got underway. Afterward, Jean lingered in her chair, waiting for the crown to dissipate, hoping to maybe get a moment alone with the actress. She never expected Christina to approach *her.*

"I remember you from this morning," Christina said with a sweet smile. "Are you enjoying the convention so far?" Christina asked.

"Oh, yes, very much," Jean jumped up. She was stunned that the actress had asked her, rather than the other way around. "How about you?"

"It's been lovely so far." Christina's brilliant eyes sparkled as she spoke.

"Are you planning on going to any of the parties tonight?" Jean asked.

"Not tonight, no, I'm pretty beat," Christina said with a stifled yawn that was so incredibly adorable it almost made up for the disappointing answer to the question.

"That's too bad…" Jean began.

"But I'll be sure to on Saturday," Christina said, and Jean perked up. Christina smiled at her. "If you'll be around," she added, and Jean nearly fainted from happiness.

"Yes," was all she could manage to say; the way Christina was looking at her made Jean feel all warm and melty inside.

"Good." Christina lightly squeezed Jean's arm. "I'll see you around then."

Jean watched Christina walk off toward the doorway in a blissful fog. *She touched me. She* flirted *with me.* Jean had to sit down, or she might actually faint. *I can't believe this is really real.*

Chapter 7:
Harmony

Friday 4:30pm

Harmony watched out of the corner of her eye as Christina chatted with the frustratingly gorgeous cosplayer. Next to her, Harmony's new *buddy* Jeff was prattling on about God knows what. Ever since they'd shared pizza on Thursday, he'd been following her around like a little lost puppy. Harmony wasn't overly bothered; the guy had very little self-awareness, so he didn't get her this-conversation-is-over hints, but he also didn't seem to notice when she barely paid attention to what he said. Besides, Harmony knew she wasn't always great at picking up social cues either.

But even from across the room, Harmony was picking up on some heavy cues—signs that suggested Christina was *flirting* with the cosplay chick. The way Christina smiled and leaned close to the auburn-haired fan made Harmony's tummy rumble with envy. She strained to hear their conversation over Jeff's endless chatter.

"But I'll be sure to on Saturday," Christina said. *Be sure to what?* Harmony wondered.

"Have you read the Wheel of Time series?" Jeff's insistent question interrupted Harmony's eaves-dropping.

"What?" Harmony looked at him, her brain slowly catching up and processing his words. "Oh, no. I started to, but I wasn't that into—"

"You really should—" Jeff began what Harmony could tell was going to be an impassioned speech. She shook her head, whipping her curls violently back and forth.

"Nope, nope, nuh-un, no thanks," she said, cutting him off. "I get that people love it, but I've got plenty of things on my list."

"Oh, okay," Jeff let it drop.

They sat in silence until Harmony's watch buzzed. She glanced at it. "Crap, I have to get to a panel I'm on." She cast one last longing glance at Christina. Harmony had really wanted to chat with Christina again, but between Jeff, Jean, and the time constraint, that was not going to happen here and now. Harmony turned and scurried out of the room, shuffling down the hall in her Hufflepuff-clad feet toward the "Ask a Scientist" panel.

"Ask a Scientist" was one of Harmony's favorite events to participate in at the convention. She enjoyed being asked questions and having a platform to dispel common misconceptions about her field. Today's iteration wasn't one of the better ones. Nevertheless, the time passed quickly.

When it ended, Harmony meandered back toward the consuite. Running into Gabby along the way.

"How was 'ask a scientist?'" Gabby asked. "I'm sorry I didn't go to it this year, but there was another one I just had to check out."

"Oh, that's fine." Harmony waved her hand dismissively; she didn't care if Gabby attended the panel; Gabby listened to her prattle on about physics all the time. "It went okay. I didn't get to say much; most of the discussion ended up centering on the biological sciences."

"So, no 'neutrino beam' jokes?" Gabby asked with a grin.

"Not a one." Harmony shook her head. "Honestly, I barely talked at all."

"Ah, well, that's too bad. You make such great faces when you're talking physics." Gabby's grin broadened as she widened her eyes and bounced on her toes in imitation of Harmony's nerdy exuberance.

"Yeah, yeah." Harmony poked her in the side. "I did get to learn some cool new facts. Did you know that prairie dogs have their own sort of language? They differentiate approaching predators and communicate that with different sounds." Harmony lifted her nose and held her hands up like paws. "Hawk incoming!" she squeaked.

"That reminds me of that 'elephants and bees' meme," Gabby said.

"Huh?"

"'Why don't humans have a specific noise that means 'there are bees here, let's leave immediately'? Why are elephants more advanced than us?'" Gabby quoted. "'We do have a specific noise. It sounds like this: *There are bees here, let's leave immediately.*'"

"Hah. Right," Harmony chuckled. "Speaking of memes, we also got into quite a heated debate over the theory of genetic memory and how much one could extrapolate over a study on goldfish."

"What now?" Gabby asked, but Harmony didn't feel like retelling the whole thing.

"Nevermind. Hey, did you know tardigrades can withstand vacuum when hibernating?" Harmony asked. She didn't wait for an answer. "Oh, or that banana slugs are born hermaphroditic? When they have sex, they have to chew off at least one of the penes—"

"Sounds like you had fun," Gabby loudly interrupted, apparently not interested in information regarding banana slug reproduction. "But what's next?"

"I don't know," Harmony responded. They both pulled out pocket programs; Harmony scanned the schedule. There weren't any events that jumped out at her.

"Nothing, I guess," she said.

"Would you want to go to the dealer's room with me?" Gabby asked, shoving her program in her back pocket and looking at Harmony.

"Sure, why not," Harmony agreed with a quick shrug. She'd already been through the dealer's room once, but it never hurt to take another stroll through and see what caught Gabby's eye.

"Are you feeling any better today regarding your break-up with Tammy?" Harmony asked as they walked through the crowds.

"No, if anything, I feel worse. She texted me this morning. I think I might have to leave early and go back and talk to her in person," Gabby said with a shake of her head.

"Does she want to get back together?"

"No... I don't know. It's confusing because Tam basically said that she might have thought about getting back together if I hadn't made the 'selfish choice' to come here to JanCon. But like, that choice had already been made, and I made it *because* she broke up with me." Gabby's shoulders sagged as she spoke. "I have to wonder if she's only saying it because she knows there'll be no consequences for her, but it will still make me feel bad."

"That's a pretty shitty thing to do. And if she is doing it on purpose?" Harmony blew a loud raspberry. "I mean, I know you love her, but she's kind of a total butthole." Harmony put an arm around Gabby's shoulders and squeezed. "You deserve better treatment than that."

"Yeah," Gabby said softly.

Does Gabby believe that she's worth more than what Tammy's giving her? Harmony wasn't convinced she did. *Tammy deserves a kick in the teeth.* Manipulative relationship tactics were something Harmony just could not abide. Laying traps and tricks for somebody you care about seemed illogical, counter-productive, and just plain mean. *How can I take Gabby's mind off of her stupid, buttface ex?*

"I've got an idea," Harmony chirped. "I saw the *hottest* corset in the dealer's room. Let's go dress you up all sexy-like."

"And post pictures to social media just to piss Tammy off?" Gabby's eyes brightened with excitement, and she steepled her fingers.

"Oh, um, I hadn't thought about it like that—" Harmony began.

"Doesn't matter, I'm in!" Gabby grinned as she grabbed Harmony's hand and began pulling her toward the dealer's room at a trot. Harmony laughed as she went along with her friend.

The dealer's room was much more crowded than it had been earlier in the day—throngs of fans filled the space, crowding around the different booths and stands. Harmony pointed out the black silk corset she'd noticed earlier, and Gabby immediately pulled it down to try on. Harmony helped her lace up the garment and then stepped back.

"Oh, it looks so good!" Harmony said, clapping her hands together.

"It does," Gabby agreed, as she looked at herself in the shop mirror. "I wants it, precious."

"It totally suits you," Harmony said as she snapped a few pictures with Gabby's phone. While Harmony scrolled through the photos, Gabby slowly unlaced the corset and put it back on its hanger.

"Aren't you gonna buy it?" Harmony asked.

"I don't know; it's expensive," Gabby said, looking thoughtfully at the corset. "Although I did just get that bonus at work…"

"Go for it!" Harmony encouraged her. Harmony didn't have the body or the money for the corset, but she liked the idea of living vicariously through her friend. Before Gabby could make up her mind, the hotel fire alarm began to blare. Harmony clapped her hands over her ears.

"You don't think it could really be a fire, do you?" Gabby asked over the din as she set down the corset and began to move in the direction of the exit.

"It's improbable but not impossible, I suppose," Harmony replied. They walked out of the dealer's room toward the front of the hotel. All around them, legions of fans did the same. Harmony squinted at the blinking fire alarms. "If it were a fire, I would think the sprinklers would go off," she said, pointing to the ceiling.

"They'd better not!" Gabby squealed, covering her head. "I do not need an indoor shower, thank you very much."

"Aren't most showers indoors?" Harmony quipped.

"Shut up. You know what I meant." Gabby lightly shoved Harmony, who laughed as she stumbled forward toward the hotel's front doors.

"It doesn't look like you're going to be able to avoid that shower," Harmony said, pointing. Outside it was raining; it wasn't exactly pouring, but it certainly wasn't a light sprinkling either.

"Son of a bitch," Gabby groaned. "If we go out there, we're going to get soaked."

"Worse things have happened," Harmony said with a shrug.

"Harmony, you're not even wearing any shoes," Gabby pointed out. Harmony looked down; she wiggled her toes.

"Ah, yes, that is not optimal," Harmony agreed. *Did I even remember to bring extra socks?* Harmony wasn't sure that she had. *Certainly not optimal.* But there was nothing to be done about it. The hotel staff were quite clear in their directions: the fans of JanCon had to exit the building.

The space under the hotel's small awning was quickly overcrowded. People courteously made room for those cosplayers whose costumes would be devastated by the rain, such as a blue-skinned Twi'lek and a foam-and-cardboard Gundam. Harmony was grateful that she and Gabby had a place there, even if it was a tight fit. The Twi'lek—a scantily clad woman whose killer body was painted bright blue—was mere inches away. *If I bump into her, will the blue run off on me?* The woman was quite beautiful. Harmony *really* wanted to ask her if the body paint was sex-proof—the idea of fondling those blue boobs was enticing. But she didn't think she could ask that question without sounding creepy, so she kept it to herself. The Twi'lek woman caught her gaze, and Harmony grinned awkwardly at her.

"I hope we can go back inside soon; you must be freezing," Harmony said quickly, hoping she hadn't been caught staring at her cerulean cleavage.

"I am," the Twi'lek confirmed in a high sweet voice, seemingly unbothered by Harmony's wandering eyes. She sighed. "This is really harshing my squee."

"Yeah," Harmony agreed. "But it could be worse. At least we aren't directly in the rain."

"Thank the Force," the woman nodded. "This took me hours," she continued, but Harmony wasn't listening anymore.

Over the Twi'lek's blue shoulder, out in the rain, Harmony had spotted a familiar figure standing in the middle of the hotel lot, alone and drenched. *Francesca.* At a distance, the cosplayer bore such a perfect resemblance to the character that Harmony almost felt as if she were watching an episode of High School Bites. Francesca hugged herself against the cold; she looked absolutely miserable. For a moment, Harmony forgot her jealousy, and her heart went out to the woman. Drops of water were rolling down Francesca's face like tears; dye dripped from her long hair, creating blood-red blossoms on her white t-shirt. Her flawless skin was covered in goosebumps, and she was shivering violently. *Poor Francesca.*

Their eyes met, and Francesca's lips curled in an unfriendly snarl, showing off one tiny white fang. *That's not Francesca.* Harmony looked away, her sympathy for the woman dropping precipitously. She huddled closer to Gabby. Some sinister part of Harmony was glad that the cosplayer's costume was being wrecked by the rain. *Maybe Christina won't pay so much attention to her if she doesn't look like Francesca.* Although Harmony suspected the woman would still be unreasonably attractive in whatever she wore, any slight shift in Harmony's advantage was welcome.

She risked another glance at would-be Francesca. *I shouldn't be glad she's so unhappy. It's highly unlikely she wants Christina like I do,* Harmony told herself. She debated offering to squeeze the cosplayer in under the awning. But before she could act, the doors opened, and the hotel staff beckoned the crowds inside. By the time the chaos of reentry died down, Francesca was nowhere to be seen.

Chapter 8:
Jean

Friday, 6:55pm

Jean made it back to her room wet and shivering from standing in the ice-cold rain. *Stupid fire alarm.* Her hands were shaking so intensely she could barely use her keycard to open the door. She stepped into the dim room and looked at herself in the large mirror. She was an absolute mess. Her soaked shirt was almost pornographically translucent, and her once-perfect makeup ran down her face, making her look like she belonged in a Salvidor Dali painting. But worst of all, her wet hair, which hung limp around her shoulders, had bled. She turned in the mirror; the back of her perfect Paddington High t-shirt was now streaked with red dye.

"Jian ta de gui," she swore, once again mentally kicking herself for using cheap store-bought hair color. She took a few deep breaths. *There's nothing I can do about it now; it's not the end of the world.* She still had the other costume for tomorrow, and she was too tired to deal with cosplay anymore tonight. The moment that fire alarm had begun blaring, the cosplay energy bubble surrounding Jean had burst. She still wanted to enjoy the convention, but outside of the spotlight of cosplay.

I may as well shower. Her teeth were still chattering with cold, and a hot shower was just the thing to help. She turned on the water so that it could warm up while she undressed.

Jean peeled off her wet shirt, revealing the plain white bra beneath, which fortunately appeared unaffected by the seeping dye. She quickly pulled it off, hanging it up to dry. Her nipples were hard, her skin covered in goosebumps. But the spray of the hotel's dual-headed shower was steaming now, so Jean shimmied out of her wet shorts and panties and climbed in. It took a long time for the heat of the water to penetrate her body and thaw her frozen core. When she finally stepped out of the shower, her fingers were wrinkled, and her skin was bright pink from the heat. But at least she was warm.

Jean dried and dressed in her most comfortable oversized sweats. She had no desire to fix her hair or put on makeup. Besides, she didn't have time if she wanted to get to the dealer's room before it closed for the night.

She'd been thinking about the sexy black corset all day and decided buying it would bring her spirits up after the sad demise of her High School Bites tee. Jean pulled the hood of her sweatshirt up over her wet hair and looked in the mirror. *Goodbye, beautiful, bold Francesca. Hello, plain old Jean.* With a sigh, she grabbed her backpack and left the room.

Jean moved through the throngs of convention-goers as if invisible. Nobody looked twice at her as she walked by. Jean wove her way across the dealer's room toward the tall racks of the costume shop. Her eyes quickly scanned the display. She caught sight of the corset and grinned.

"Huzzah," she whispered to herself. *It's still here.* She plucked it down and took out her credit card to pay before the shop clerk could offer to help. This was how Jean preferred to shop: with targeted precision and minimal conversation. Transaction complete, Jean tucked her purchase carefully into her bag and scurried off, glowing with satisfaction.

What next? Jean consulted her schedule. Everything she had so carefully planned had been thrown off by the rain and her subsequent need to shower and change. She flipped through the schedule, considering her options. If her mother were there, she would have leaned toward filking—participating in fannish music circles. But left to her own devices, Jean preferred visual art. After a quick consultation of the hotel map, Jean took off in the direction of the art show.

JanCon's art show was a maze of metal racks, on which hung a wide array of drawings, paintings, and photography. Convention art ranged widely—sketches of spaceships, dystopian pop art, portraits of buxom women lounging with dragons, a mix of the fantastically unique and entirely cliché. Tables lined the walls around the room's periphery, covered with statues, knitwear, jewelry, and other three-dimensional art pieces. Some of the items were for display only. Still, much of it was available for sale either through silent auction or to 'quick buy' immediately for a higher price than the opening bid amount.

Jean took a moment to assess the room's layout, always looking for the most efficient and comprehensive path, before slowly weaving her way through the displays. There were several popular artists selling prints she'd seen at conventions back east. The atmosphere of JanCon had already been comfortably familiar, but seeing these specific images brought on a sudden feeling of being home. The sensation was acute and sweetly painful. *I should have done this years ago.* Jean stood before the works of an artist she'd admired for ages, studying the well-known images of cat and dragon.

"Hello, Magnus. Hello, Loki," she whispered. Tears came, unexpected, to her eyes. She hadn't realized how lonely and homesick she'd been until she'd seen these two old friends. She wiped tears from her cheeks and pulled her hood closer around her face. It was embarrassing, such an overly emotional reaction to something so simple. *I need to make real friends. Crying over art is just pathetic*, she scolded herself. Jean placed a high bid on one of her favorite prints and moved on.

Once she was sure that she'd seen everything and that she wasn't about to break down again, Jean made her way from the art show to the consuite. She needed food, and she strongly desired alcohol. She picked up a drink—something pinkish, sweet, and strong—along with a banana, some cheese, and a small basket of popcorn. *Booze, fruit, protein, and filler. The four major food groups.* Jean smiled to herself as she sat on the edge of the consuite, eating her banana. She contemplated the friendship issue. She'd prefer to connect with people while being herself, not Francesca. But she needed to find an organic way to meet them. *One does not simply acquire friends.* Jean was hardly the type to just walk up to somebody and start a conversation. Structured activity was her best option. *Board games.*

Jean finished her food and refilled her drink before traipsing down the stairs toward the wide-open gaming area. White linen-covered tables of various sizes and shapes were spread throughout the space. Two large tables in the center held stacks and stacks of games and puzzles. People occupied approximately half of the remaining tables, playing games or chatting.

Jean meandered about, glancing at the different options. She stopped to stand beside a group of fans playing a delightfully simple game of Settlers of Catan. *Oh, I haven't played Settlers in so long.* Watching the old familiar game sent a fresh wave of nostalgia and homesickness swirling through her. Worried that she might have another emotional episode, Jean quickly moved on. She sat down at an empty table and sipped her drink until the feeling passed. She considered reaching out to her parents to tell them all about JanCon. But she decided against it. She'd fill them in during her weekly call Sunday evening.

Jean sat still for a while, sipping her drink and considering her options until the alcohol had carried her into a swaying, happy stupor. *I could try to be social and join a game.* She stood, meaning to approach a group opening an Ingenious box. On her way, something else caught her eye: a thousand-piece jigsaw puzzle of Yoda carrying a bag of toys a la Santa Claus. It was half-finished and abandoned, just begging to be completed.

Sober Jean could barely resist a puzzle; tipsy Jean had no chance. She instantly forgot about being social and sat down. Jean loved puzzles—she was an addict—and she was good at them. She sat content and alone, picking out pieces and putting them together until the image was assembled. Jean snapped a picture before folding the completed puzzle neatly into its box. Only then did she remember she'd come down here to find *people* to interact with.

Come on, Jean. You have to at least try, she scolded herself, *at least a little bit*. She had plenty of friends back at her old conventions. There was no logical reason why she couldn't make friends here. No reason, other than the fact that she'd barely spoken to another human being—not since that jackwagon had quizzed her about the Wheel of Time books.

Jean stood and did a slow circuit of the room. Four young men were playing Pandemic, a group of six huddled around Empire Builder, and a couple older guys were packing up to head to the bar. But no groups looking to add players.

Feeling somewhat discouraged, Jean sat back down alone at a small table. She pulled a few of her own games from her bag. Set, Fluxx, and Zar—all simple, easy to carry around, popular, and social. Jean set Fluxx and Zar out on the table like bait—she needed other players for those two. But she could play Set all on her own. It wouldn't be all that exciting, but it was something. She laid out the cards.

Set. Flip, flip, flip. Set. Flip, flip, flip. Aside from one guy who came by, pointed out a set, and walked off, Jean's ploy failed to draw in potential friends. When she'd exhausted the Set deck, she packed it away. *Why do I suck at meeting new people?* Jean sighed and pulled out the Zar deck. *I'll give myself seven shuffles, and if nobody comes by in that time, I need to find something else to do.*

Chapter 9:
Harmony

Friday, 8:57pm

After a few drinks at the bar with her friends, Harmony wandered down to the gaming area alone, looking for a bit of fun. She was happily tipsy as she meandered around, appreciating the atmosphere and the sensation of her new, *dry* Star Wars socks on the thin hotel carpeting. The evening had been pleasant after their unfortunate and unexpected fire drill. But she was restless now and in need of mental stimulation beyond aimless chit-chat. Games would be just the thing.

A few yards away, a woman dressed in a plain gray hoodie sat alone at a table shuffling cards. *Oh! Zar cards!* Harmony loved Zar. It was fast-paced and cut-throat while also loaning itself to entertaining social interactions. She liked to compare it to Uno on speed. When she saw the woman with the cards, Harmony immediately bounded over to the table.

"Can I join you?" she asked the woman.

"If you want to," a familiar voice responded. Harmony had to do a double take. *It's that cosplayer again.* She hadn't recognized the woman, dressed as she was. She'd washed off all her makeup and hidden her shining auburn hair under the hood of her oversized sweatshirt. She'd seemingly washed off all her confidence along with the makeup because instead of her perfect posture, she was slumped, her shoulders hunched like she was turning inward, hiding within herself. But when she looked up at Harmony with her deep blue eyes, Harmony could see all the radiant beauty was still there—just as she had suspected, it would be.

Looking at her made Harmony's stomach twist, although she couldn't have said why. There was something about this woman that continued to make Harmony uncomfortable. Nonetheless, she pulled out the chair and sat down across the table.

"It's you! I didn't know that. You look different from before," Harmony blurted out before she could think better of it.

Frowning slightly, the woman put down the cards and shoved her hands in the pocket of her hoodie.

"I changed," she muttered.

"I mean, duh," Harmony said with a laugh. "I didn't think you actually *were* Francesca."

The woman looked back up at Harmony. "No, I'm not, *Harmony*," she said with a sudden bite to her words. "I'm Jean."

"I know," Harmony lied while mentally slapping herself in the forehead. *Why don't I ever remember people's names?* It was one of the social niceties she knew she needed to improve upon. Harmony couldn't read Jean's expression. Her symmetrical features were perfectly still as she returned to shuffling the cards. *Why does she dislike me? It doesn't make sense; she doesn't even know me.*

"Harmony is my real name, by the way," Harmony said, tapping her badge.

"I never assumed it wasn't," Jean replied warily.

Harmony shrugged. "Sometimes people wonder if it's just a moniker I use at conventions, but no, my mom is just a huge music nerd. My sister's name is Melody, and my brother is Johann."

"Johann? For Bach?" Jean asked.

"Nope. Strauss. Mom loves a good waltz." Harmony swayed as she hummed a little *An der schönen blauen Donau.* She grinned at Jean. "I have the dorkiest parents on earth."

"I doubt that," Jean said; she didn't elaborate, and they both fell silent.

Harmony drummed her fingers on the table, trying to think of something to say. "So, Zar," Harmony said, pointing to the deck in Jean's hand. "Have you played that before?"

Jean glowered at her, and Harmony felt her cheeks warm. "Oh, right, of course, you probably have since you're shuffling the cards...." Harmony cleared her throat. "So, play much?"

"Yes," Jean snipped.

"Oh, cool, I love Zar. That's why I came over. Want me to go grab a couple people, and we can start up a game?" Harmony offered.

Jean hesitated. Her face was pretty but absolutely unreadable, like a decommissioned android—beautiful but blank. Harmony was on the cusp of repeating her offer when Jean nodded. "Sure, that would be fun," she said. Her lips turned up in a small, reluctant smile.

"Excellent!" Harmony popped up out of her chair. "Be right back." She bounded across the gaming room to where a cluster of familiar folks lingered. Some of them were playing Ingenious, but others were clearly just standing around.

"Hello!" she said as she hopped into place next to them, grinning.

"Hello!" Mac said back with a frantic wave, matching her perky greeting with his own brand of enthusiasm.

"Anybody up for a game of Zar? We have two and a table over there," Harmony pointed.

"I'll play!" Mac replied quickly.

"I'm going to bed soon, but I'll watch for a while," Ginny said with a yawn.

"One more? Four is the optimal number..." Harmony looked around the group.

"Okay, if you wait for me to run to get another drink, I'm in," Chris said, standing.

"Oh, get me a drink too?" Harmony asked, leaning on Chris's shoulder and smiling sweetly up at him with her most look-how-cute-I-am smile. It was a pretty safe bet that he would say "yes" when she looked at him like that.

"Okay," he sighed in feigned resignation and gave her a quick squeeze. "What are you drinking?"

"Whatever. I'm not picky, as long as it's alcoholic," Harmony shrugged.

"You'd better be careful; he's going to take you too literally," Ginny warned with a laugh, "Better add some conditions, or he's going to come back with a cup of plain cheap Bacardi."

Harmony looked at Chris, and he smirked. If he hadn't been planning on pulling some trick like that before, he certainly was now.

Harmony scrunched up her face and stuck out her tongue. "Better not!" she said. "Okay, said drink must be prepared as is intended to be drank."

"Aren't all drinks intended to be drank? If they weren't, they wouldn't *be* drinks, technically. Would they?" Chris said, just to be a smart-ass.

"Not necessarily. The *ability* to be drunk is not the same as *the intention* to be."

"I have the ability *and* intention to be drunk," Mac chimed in.

"What I'm saying is," Harmony continued. "If you use cheap liquor, that means you must use an appropriate mixer."

"Who gets to define appropriate?" Chris asked, his smirk spreading into an impish grin.

Harmony stuck out her bottom lip in an exaggerated pout. She crossed her arms across her chest. "Be nice to me," she said.

Chris laughed and kissed her cheek. "I will. Don't worry," he said. "Be right back with your drink, beautiful."

"Thanks!" Harmony's pout was instantly replaced by a wide smile. All joking aside, she trusted Chris. He'd always been sweet to her.

Harmony turned and skipped back to the table. Jean was still there; she'd stopped shuffling and was sitting, examining her short nails. Her fingers were long and slender, and even though she wasn't doing anything other than picking at her cuticles, somehow, the movements of Jean's fingers seemed graceful. *Her hands look so soft. Like Christina's.* Harmony dismissed the thought.

"I'm back!" she said. "Sorry that took so long, but I come bearing players!" Harmony dropped back into her seat opposite Jean. "This is Mac and Ginny. Chris will be here soon, too—once he fetches drinks."

"No drinks on the Zar table," Jean said cooly.

"Oh, I know. We'll be good. Go ahead and deal for four players." Harmony gestured to the cards.

"Four?" Jean's eyes moved, and Harmony could tell she was counting them, and the numbers didn't add up.

"Oh, Ginny isn't playing," Harmony explained. Ginny nodded and pulled a chair up behind Mac, leaving the fourth chair open for Chris. Silently, Jean began to deal. All the quiet this woman was throwing at her was disquieting. Harmony didn't like it.

"Did you shuffle seven times?" she asked, mainly to make conversation.

"Of course I did," Jean muttered.

"You have to if you want them properly randomized," Mac added.

"I *know*," Jean snapped; she finished dealing and slapped the remaining deck down hard on the center of the table. Harmony jumped. She wasn't used to games of Zar starting out this tense. Sometimes they *got* tense if one player felt picked on or had a run of bad luck, but this Jean lady was as prickly as a cactus, and they hadn't even picked up their cards. *No 'who dealt this shit' jokes for her. She might actually take it personally.*

Harmony and Mac exchanged glances; Harmony shrugged. She, Mac, and Ginny talked amongst themselves until Chris arrived, drinks in hand. Harmony quickly gulped down a couple mouthfuls of con punch and coughed.

"Shit, that's strong," Harmony wheezed as the cheap vodka burned her throat.

"You said I needed a mixer; you did not specify a mixer to alcohol ratio," Chris pointed out with an impish grin. Harmony laughed and sipped cautiously at the drink once more before placing it under her chair.

"Chis, this is Jean; Jean, Chris." Harmony waved a hand between the two of them.

"A pleasure to meet you," Chris said in that voice he used when he was trying to be flirtatious. *It might be interesting to see how Jean responds to him.* Chris was fairly charismatic. *If Jean shows interest in him, maybe that'll mean she isn't a rival for Christina after all.* Harmony scrutinized Jean's face. She didn't seem impressed with Chris so far. *Not that any of that means anything anyway. He could just not be her type, and even if he was, she could be bi. Don't bi-erase yourself, Harmony,* she chastised.

If Harmony wanted to find out this Jean chick's thoughts about her beloved Christina, she would have to do more than watch her interact with Chris. She was going to have to actually *say* something. Harmony chewed the inside of her cheek in thought as she picked up her cards.

"Jean's a big High School Bites fan," Harmony said. "She was *all over* Christina Darlington earlier today."

"Maybe she's hot on her like you," Chris teased, playing perfectly into Harmony's plan. Harmony glanced at Jean. Was that the hint of a blush? *Shit, she might actually be into Christina.* Harmony did *not* like that one bit. *What chance do I have against somebody who looks like her?*

Chapter 10:
Jean

Jean gritted her teeth and kept her eyes glued to the colorful peacock card in her hand. *All over her? What is it with this lady?* It wasn't a surprise that Harmony was 'hot on' Christina, she'd practically thrown herself at the actress all afternoon, but Jean didn't know why Harmony was being such a twat about it.

"You should have seen Jean before, Chris," Harmony's voice dripped with faux-sweetness. "She had the whole cosplay thing *down*. It was really impressive. I'm not that type of fan; I tried cosplay a couple times, but I just don't have the body for it like Jean does."

Chris, a barrel-chested man with thinning blonde hair, looked Jean up and down as if trying to judge the body she'd hidden in her baggy sweats. Jean felt her ears burn as she continued to stare at her cards. Harmony was looking at her, too; she could feel both of their eyes on her. Jean didn't like this type of attention. The scrutiny she was under now had nothing to do with her skills as a costumer, only the body she was born with. And she hated that.

On top of her discomfort, she was hurt by Harmony's casual assumption of what type of fan she was. *She thinks I'm just some airhead cosplayer.* Harmony didn't know that nearly every wall in Jean's apartment was covered in bookshelves. She didn't know that Jean had been reading everything from Asimov to Zhan since childhood or that she loved writing fanfic and playing board games. Jean had a body for costumes, that's all that Harmony saw, and she *judged* her for it. It didn't matter that Harmony was *gorgeous*—with her bobbing curls, full breasts, and beaming smile—or that she clearly had people falling all over her, trying to get her attention. That somehow didn't *count*.

Jean was conventionally, *mundanely* beautiful. Therefore, there's no way she could be the type of fan that would read or game or fit in at a convention outside of prancing about in cosplay. *It's not like I've said anything that would contradict her assumptions. But I haven't said anything to affirm them either. It's so unfair. I bet Harmony never assumed frumpy little Ginny was anything shy of a full-fledged geek.* Jean felt the familiar burn of frustrated tears at the back of her throat and wished she had something to drink to help push it down.

"Did you enjoy Christina's panels?" Harmony asked.

"Of course," Jean replied, straightening and forcing herself to meet Harmony's eye. "But I also I quite enjoyed the author guest of honor panels as well. Did you attend any of those?" she asked.

Harmony seemed surprised, but she quickly caught herself and gave Jean a nonchalant shrug. "Naw. I'd never even heard of him. It's Charlie McGillicuddy or something, right?"

"Charles Macalester," Jean corrected.

Harmony shrugged again. "MaTato-MaTahto."

Jean could help but smirk. "So, I take it you haven't read any of his books." It felt nice to have something up on proud little Harmony.

"They're on my list…" Harmony hesitated a moment before taking a breath and plastering on a big, bright smile. "But no. I'm a classics girl; I don't always keep up with the new trendier stuff."

Jean smiled back. "That's too bad," she said, blinking at Harmony. "There are some interesting ways you can see him draw on the classics in his Cold Star series."

"Oh, totally," Mac, the tall man with a long greasy ponytail, agreed. "I really like Rami's storyline, how it weaves around the others."

Jean smiled genuinely at him. "Yes, me too. Don't you think the way he develops characters is reminiscent of—"

"Let's start the game!" Harmony interrupted. Jean shot her a cold look. She'd finally thought maybe one of these people might want to really *talk* to her, but Mac and all the others followed Harmony's lead like a flock of trained pigeons, and the game got underway. It felt like every time Jean began to gain purchase in the conversation, Harmony would block her with inside jokes and little spotlight-stealing theatrics. She giggled prettily when she made players draw cards, bounced proudly in her seat after slapping down a match, and let out cute little pouty huffs when others matched her. Jean could understand why people were drawn to her. *I could never compete with her for anybody's attention.* Slowly Jean gave up even trying to engage the others in more than basic gameplay.

The game attracted a couple more players and spectators as they played. After the fourth hand, one of the spectators offered to fetch drinks for Harmony and her friends. He didn't ask Jean; he barely looked at her. Jean looked down at her feet where her empty cup sat. *Would I have trusted this random guy to get me a drink, even if he had offered?* She knew she wouldn't have. But it still stung that she hadn't been asked.

Jean sobered up while the others grew increasingly tipsy. The only upside to being a social outsider was that her reflexes routinely outperformed the others in her more alert state. She won hand after hand, soundly beating them all at the fast-paced game.

"No fair, you trounced us too quickly. Let's play again," Harmony sulked, her plump bottom lip pushed out. Jean couldn't pretend that she didn't notice how wicked sexy Harmony was when she did that, but it just made Jean more bitter.

"No, I think I'm going to call it a night." Jean shook her head.

"You know what the problem is," Mac said, ignoring Jean's decline. "Is that I'm too hungry. I gotta get my blood sugar up, then maybe I'll get a match in before Wonder Woman here."

"Okay, let's take a quick break for provisions, then one more round?" Harmony suggested.

"No, really. I'm tired, I'm going to bed," Jean stood up.

Harmony looked at her, stunned—as if nobody had ever said 'no' to her before. "It's so early, though!" Harmony protested, her eyebrows knit and lips pursed in a plaintive expression that would have made Jean weak in the knees if she hadn't already been so irritated.

"Goodnight, Harmony," Jean said firmly. "Excuse me, these are my cards." She picked up the deck of cards from the table, packed them into their box, and shoved them into her backpack. Jean began to walk off, but Harmony followed her.

"Could we at least borrow your cards?" Harmony asked.

Annoyance crawled like a line of ants up Jean's back, and she hunched her shoulders. "I don't want to lose them," Jean replied tartly as she continued toward the elevators.

"I promise I'll give them back tomorrow," Harmony persisted, staying on Jean's heels. "If you don't want to stay up—"

"We're not *friends*," Jean snapped, turning to give Harmony a sharp look before shoving her hands in her pockets and picking up her pace. "I don't owe you anything. Leave me alone."

"Aw, come on, we could be friends. Stay and play, and we could be friends." Harmony implored.

How is she not noticing how little I want to do with her right now? Why won't she leave me alone? "No."

"Why don't you like me?" Harmony asked with a maddeningly cute little '*huff*' that must have gotten Harmony her way a million times before. It grated on Jean's nerves. Everything about this woman seemed to set off a reaction in her.

She turned to glare at Harmony. "Because I don't like the way you act toward me," Jean growled.

If Harmony even noticed Jean's acerbic tone, she wasn't cowed. "Act like what?" Harmony asked with a feigned innocence that made Jean's blood boil.

"Like you're a bigger fan than me," Jean said bluntly. "You look at me like I'm a *mundane*, a muggle in a costume, but I'm not—"

"I never said that you were!" Harmony interrupted with a squeak.

"You don't have to say it with words; your actions speak clearly for you!" Jean all but shouted. "You don't include me like you do the others—"

"That is *false*." Harmony crossed her arms, pushing her ample chest up in a way that was impossible not to notice. She gave Jean a defiant look. "We were *just* playing Zar! I want you to come back."

"You want my *cards* back." Jean narrowed her eyes on Harmony's. "At best, you want another player to make the game work. That's *it*. Interaction is not the same as inclusion, you know."

"Woah, you're talking about levels of social awareness that I just don't have." Harmony uncrossed her arms and put up her hands defensively. "I'm a physicist; I operate on simple facts." She pointed at Jean. "Fact: I approached *you*."

"Counter 'fact': you didn't recognize me," Jean shot back.

Harmony shook her head, her curls bouncing wildly with the motion. "That's irrelevant," she insisted. "After I identified you, I proceeded to ask you to play with me."

"Wrong," Jean corrected. "You asked *before* you identified me. And what you asked was if you could join me."

"What's the difference?" Harmony asked.

Jean rolled her eyes. Wasn't it obvious? *Does she think I'm stupid?* "As soon as you saw who I was, it was like you forgot that I had been the one with the cards in the first place!" Jean said, incredulous. "You asked if I'd ever played Zar while I was shuffling my own damn Zar deck!"

"That seems like splitting hairs..." Harmony objected, but her voice had lost some of its former certainty.

Jean took advantage of the hesitation; she was sick of the way she'd been treated all night, and she was going to make Harmony understand that. "You never included me; you didn't offer me a drink, even though my cup was empty—"

"What cup? I didn't see a cup!" Harmony protested.

"It was *off* the table, *where it belonged*," Jean growled. "And forget about the stupid cup. It's not about the *drink*. My point is that you didn't ask about *me* at all! You ignored me, you interrupted me, you talked *around* me. The only reason you're chasing me now is that I have the cards," Jean stuck out her lip in an exaggerated imitation of Harmony's pout. "*But you still want to play*," she whined.

"That's not true…" Harmony hesitated again, her voice wavering.

"You continue to treat me like an outsider. Never mind that I killed you at Zar or that I actually know who the guests of honor are *aside* from Christina when you clearly *don't*." Jean took a deep breath; she suddenly felt a burning need to let Harmony know just how *wrong* her previous assumptions had been. "This isn't my first con, you know!" Jean continued, her voice rising. "I spent my first convention *inside my mother's uterus*. And my second in her arms. They may have been cons back east and not *this* con, but I'd bet hard money that I've been a part of fandom before you even *knew* what 'fandom' was."

"Now you're saying... what? That you're a bigger geek than me because your parents brought you to things I had to discover *on my own*?" Harmony countered, incredulous.

"I'm saying you don't get to jump in and start gatekeeping—"

"I'm not *gatekeeping*!" Harmony squealed.

Jean ignored Harmony's protests; she still had a point to make. "You know that guy, *Jeff*, actually tried to *quiz* me. I saw you talk to him. Did he quiz *you*?" Jean raised her eyebrows at Harmony.

Harmony gaped at her for a moment. "No. What? I don't know." Harmony opened and closed her mouth a few times. "But who cares? That's irrelevant. How does what *he* said to you mean that *I'm* gatekeeping? If I'm not very much mistaken, I am not Jeff."

"Well, you're not helping anything," Jean growled.

"I'm sorry you felt that way, but I didn't mean anything by it. Come on, give me a do-over. We could be friends—"

"No, thank you." Jean turned to walk away.

"So, you're just going to take your ball and go home then?" Harmony asked.

"Exactly," Jean said. "Now, if you'll stop following me, I'm going to bed."

"Fine. See you around." Harmony replied with a chill in her voice that Jean hadn't previously heard from her.

Jean looked back just in time to see Harmony turn on her heel and walk briskly back toward the gaming room. Jean could feel the burn of unshed tears at the back of her throat.

Nice. Way to make friends, Jean, she chided herself. *People just love being called out, after all.* Jean clenched her teeth; her pulse throbbed in her temples. *Harmony is obnoxious, but I didn't have to "take my ball and go home" like that.* Jean shook her arms out and willed herself to relax as she waited for the elevator. Jean's mind replayed the conversation. Harmony had been shocked by her accusation. *Come on, you know she wasn't excluding you on purpose; it's just how people like her are.* That didn't make it right, but Jean knew she was never going to find her place in the local fannish community if she always pushed people away or snapped at them for things they didn't even realize they were doing.

Jean stepped into the elevator and pushed the button. When she arrived at her floor and stepped out, a group of con-goers took her place in the elevator—headed back down to the games and parties on the floors below. A sharp pang of loneliness penetrated Jean's chest. *What am I doing up here?* Jean stood in the hallway, considering. She could still go back down; it was early yet. She rolled the thought over in her head and felt the weight of exhaustion on her limbs as she did.

okay if I turn in early tonight; I'll make up for it tomorrow.

Chapter 11:
Harmony

Saturday, 11:42am

Harmony slowly opened her eyes, squinting at the curtains behind which sunlight peeked. Although it was generally dim in her hotel room, the glow around the edges of the covered window was enough to cause a spike of pain in her cranium. She shut her eyes again and rolled onto her back. *I am hungover.* It wasn't a shock, given that she'd drank her weight in con punch the night before. Harmony rubbed her throbbing temples; her ears were ringing, and her stomach felt painfully empty. Convention hangovers weren't necessarily rare or unexpected, but that didn't mean Harmony enjoyed them. *I should be more careful tonight.*

Tonight, Harmony had plans. Christina would be going to the parties, and that meant Harmony would be there with bells on. She'd spent last night—and much of the early morning—in the gaming area drinking and playing and generally having fun. It was a good time, save for her little altercation with Jean. Harmony felt her already aching stomach twist uncomfortably, thinking of the incident. It had been such a stupid argument. She didn't even really know Jean, she couldn't fathom why she should care what the woman thought of her, but for some reason, their fight still bothered Harmony.

Her stomach growled loudly. *Forget about Jean; I need food and caffeine, stat.* Harmony stumbled out of bed and into the shower. The hot water, coupled with a few Aspirin, dulled the pain in her head but didn't eliminate it completely. Despite being washed and dressed in clean clothes, Harmony still felt grumpy and gross when she'd left her room. She trudged downstairs to the consuite, where she poured herself a generous serving of Mountain Dew. She didn't know if her empty stomach could handle coffee, but her head desperately needed caffeine.

After a few careful sips, Harmony moved to check out the food selection. It was already pretty picked over. *This is what I get for staying up late and sleeping in.* Harmony stared longingly at the crumbs from the bagels that were no longer there. She grabbed a granola bar and stuffed it in her pocket. *Maybe there will be better food in the greenroom.*

Harmony dragged her feet down the corridor to the smaller suite. The woman sitting beside the food table eyed her suspiciously, but Harmony ignored her. With shaking hands, Harmony spread strawberry cream cheese on her onion bagel. It was not an ideal combination, but the greenroom had obviously seen its fair share of hungry visitors this morning, and this was the best she was going to get.

Harmony sat in the greenroom, gulping down soda, trying to wake up, and hoping she would magically start feeling better. She was about to give up and go back to bed when Christina stepped into the room. Her presence was a light in the darkness, allowing Harmony to climb out of her foul mood like a butterfly breaking out of a chrysalis into the sunshine.

"Hi, Christina!" Harmony said, with a level of cheer she wouldn't have thought possible a few seconds ago.

"Good morning," Christina replied, smiling back at her.

"So," Harmony began, as casually as possible. "What's your day looking like, Christina?" The question was purely social—Harmony knew Christina's schedule for the day.

"I'm just checking in before my luncheon, then I have one more panel before I'm stuck at the autograph table for the afternoon. After that, I'm judging the costume contest." She let out a half-sigh, half-laugh. "And if I'm not too tired after all of that, I'll hit the parties tonight."

"Oh, I hope you do," Harmony said with enthusiasm. "Autograph sessions are probably pretty draining, but the costume contest is fun."

"They are so draining. I mean, don't get me wrong, I love meeting fans. But the pace and be dizzying. Plus, my fingers cramp up pretty fast." Christina shook her right hand as if shaking away the very thought of her future discomfort.

"I hope your fingers don't get *too* tired," Harmony said. "You might need those later." She wiggled her eyebrows and smiled brazenly at Christina. While she may have looked confident on the outside, inside, Harmony was stunned by her own forwardness. *Oh shit, why did I say that?* Her heart seemed to freeze in her chest while she waited to see how Christina would react to her insinuation.

The actress threw her head back and laughed aloud, her slender frame shaking as she did. "Oh my God," she giggled.

Harmony's heart began to beat again, rushing blood to her face. "Sorry, maybe that was a bit…" Harmony laughed nervously along with Christina.

"No, no." Christina put a hand on Harmony's shoulder. "I appreciate the laugh." She took a deep breath and leaned closer to Harmony. "You're not wrong either," she added in a whisper, a mischievous glint in her sparkling blue eyes. "But don't worry, this isn't my first convention, you know."

"Mine either," Harmony replied softly. Christina's face was so close to her own that Harmony could smell the sweetness of her perfume mixed with the lingering scent of coffee on her breath. Harmony wanted nothing more than to kiss her right then. Her perfect pink lips were mere inches away. Harmony could almost taste them.

"Speaking of the convention," Christina said, pulling back and breaking the spell of the moment. "I should probably get to that luncheon, or I'll never be back in time for my panel."

"Oh, yeah," Harmony sputtered. "Have fun. I'll, uh, see you later."

"See you later," Christina repeated, and with a wave of the sexiest fingers that could have ever possibly existed, she turned and walked back out of the greenroom.

Harmony collapsed into a chair, her insides melting like a snowman in July. *That was some seriously heavy flirting.* Harmony felt dizzy and lightheaded; her heart was working overtime trying to pump blood to her overly-excited—and probably dehydrated—brain. Her mind was foggy—filled with thoughts of Christina and fingers and *sex*. She was so distracted that she didn't notice Mac enter the room until he poked her in the side of the head.

"You alive in there, Harmony?" he asked.

"Huh?" Harmony looked up at her friend.

"You look like a zombie," Mac commented.

Harmony stretched and stood up. "Yeah, not enough sleep." She gave Mac a once-over. He was wearing the same t-shirt as he had been last night, his eyes were glassy, and he smelled like BO. "Did *you* get any sleep at all?" Harmony asked.

Mac shook his head. "Nope, after you crashed, I got sucked into a classic Nintendo battle. I haven't even been back to my room yet."

"Yikes." Harmony let out a puff of air. "How are you still standing?"

"You know, I'm not entirely sure," Mac grinned.

Harmony shook a finger at him. "You should get some rest."

"That's why I wanted to talk to you actually," Mac said, bobbing his head. "I need to go pass out, but I'm signed up for a few volunteer shifts. I need to get covered first. Think you could help me out?"

"Sure, of course! What's the gig?" Harmony asked.

"A few hours at the reg desk," Mac said, handing her a folded piece of paper. "Then masquerade set-up."

Harmony unfolded the paper and glanced over the schedule Mac had highlighted. She winced. Taking on these tasks would mean Harmony couldn't attend either Christina's next panel *or* her signing. But her friend looked like hell, and she couldn't take back her offer just to sit in the crowd, gawking at Christina—not without feeling like an asshole. "Okay, no problem." She folded the paper back up and stuck it in her pocket.

Relief washed over Mac's face. "Thanks," he said. "And if it helps, part of setting up the for the masquerade entails working directly with Christina."

Harmony perked up. "Well, in that case, it truly is my pleasure." She gave Mac a theatrical bow. "Sleep well, my friend."

"Be seeing you," Mac replied, and with a little salute, he too walked out of the greenroom.

Not a bad deal, Harmony thought to herself as she refilled her cup of Mountain Dew, stacked her plate with snacks, and shuffled out the door and down the hall to the registration desk. She would spend the afternoon sitting around, chatting with fellow fans, and nursing her hangover, and in the evening, she'd be rewarded with another chance to talk to Christina one-on-one. *Not a bad deal at all.*

Chapter 12:
Jean

Saturday, 12:30pm

Jean wouldn't let the unsettling confrontation from the previous night derail her plans for Saturday. She proceeded as scheduled, returning to her room promptly after lunch to change into her second Francesca cosplay. Normally, Jean would have waited until the last minute before the masquerade to don her costume, but she wanted the chance to show off the dress to Christina in person. Christina would be signing autographs this afternoon, and even if it was brief, the event insured at least a few moments face-to-face with Christina.

Jean applied her makeup with painstaking care. This was the more detailed look, and she wanted it to be perfect. She studied her face in the mirror. The dark charcoal coloring around her eyes made her irises appear to be a lighter, almost royal blue. Her lips were painted with a deep burgundy lipstick. And when slightly parted, they contrasted wonderfully with her tiny white vampire fangs. *The fangs do look real; I wonder what it would feel like to kiss someone while wearing them.* Jean ran her tongue along her teeth. *Let's not get ahead of ourselves,* she admonished.

Jean turned her attention to her clothing. She slipped into the dress and zipped it up on the side. She examined her reflection in the hotel's full-length mirror. The form-flattering velvet gown matched her lipstick, striking a similarly stark contrast against her pale skin. The dress, Francesca's prom dress, was iconic and central to Jean's favorite story arch. And *wicked* sexy.

Jean was ready well in advance of Christina's signing even, but she purposefully hung back—waiting so that she could be last in line for Christina's autograph. Her hope was that doing so would give her the chance to talk to Christina for a bit afterward. The actress's eyes seemed to light up as Jean approached the table.

"Jean! I'm so glad to see you again," she said brightly.

"You are?" Jean blurted out in surprise.

Christina laughed. "Of course," she said. "How are you? Your costume is to die for."

"Well, I am supposed to be undead," Jean responded with a shrug. *Hey, stupid, you didn't even thank her for the compliment.* "And thank you," she added hastily.

Flirting was always hard for Jean, but trying to flirt across an autograph table was extra awkward.

"Did you make it?" Christina asked, standing to get a better look at the dress. She lightly touched Jean's arm, stroking the soft fabric and sending a shiver up Jean's spine. Butterflies fluttered in her chest.

"Yes, although I got a lot of help making the pattern," Jean looked down, smoothing the soft red fabric. Working with the velvet had been so stressful, but it was worth it; the dress had turned out nearly perfect.

"I'm so impressed. I love to sew, but I'm not half as talented as you," Christina said, sitting down on the table before her.

The autograph hall had emptied out; they were the only people around. When Jean realized she was truly alone with Christina for the first time, her heart rate doubled.

"I hope it's not weird to say this, Christina, but you were my first crush," Jean admitted, smiling meekly at the actress. Her cheeks warmed, and she hoped the pale Francesca makeup was keeping her face from turning as cherry red as it felt.

"Really?" Christina asked, her tone and expression encouraging.

Jean nodded. "I didn't realize it was a crush because I didn't know I was gay yet. But eventually, my mom pointed out how smitten I was."

"That is so cute." Christina's fingers trailed down Jean's arm; she squeezed Jean's hand. "I remember my first girl crush…" Christina's voice trailed off, a faint smile on her lips, her eyes unfocused, remembering.

"Who was it?" Jean asked. Christina's gaze refocused on Jean, and she smiled conspiratorially.

"Promise you won't tell anyone?" she asked.

"Of course," Jean said, her words coming out breathlessly. *Christina is going to share a secret with me? Me?*

Christina leaned closer, her fingers lightly tracing the seam on the shoulder of Jean's dress. "Lindsey," she said quietly.

"Lindsey MacMillan?" Jean asked, wide-eyed. *Francesca.*

"Yes," Christina bit her lip, her expression vulnerable and so very adorable.

Jean's mind was racing. *I knew they had chemistry. Oh my god, is that why she seems into me? Because I'm dressed like Francesca?* "Did you ever tell her?" Jean asked.

A few strands of Christina's blonde hair fell across her face as she shook her head. "No, but she figured it out. I don't know how but…" Christina trailed off.

"Teenage girls are not the most subtle creatures," Jean said, imagining how she might have acted had she worked alongside Christina in Lindsey's place. She would never have been able to keep her feelings a secret. "What did Lindsey do?" Jean couldn't help but ask. "Did anything ever… happen?"

"She was so angry and 'grossed out,'" Christina responded with a sad little sigh. "She repeatedly warned me that I'd better not 'do anything'—not that I would have; I knew she didn't like girls. She made that *abundantly* clear."

"I'm sorry," Jean whispered. Christina shook her head again, loosening more of her golden locks. Jean reached out and, with trembling fingers, tucked Christina's hair behind her ear. "That must have been hard."

"A lot of things about being a child actress were hard." Christina looked up into Jean's eyes. "But I wouldn't trade my time with her for anything. Even though she was cold to me that last year of filming, I never stopped loving her." Christina touched Jean's costume again. There was so much more Jean could read in that touch now. Christina wasn't flirting with Jean; she was flirting with the ghost of her first love. Jean didn't entirely know how she felt about that, but she wasn't about to turn away Christina's attention. Being this close with her was just too magical to resist.

"That love came through on screen. It's part of what I liked about you, or, you know, Alessia," Jean told her. "I connected with that sort of... undercurrent of unrequited love."

"You must be a very empathetic person." Christina tilted her head and looked thoughtfully at Jean.

She's looking at me now, not Lindsey. Jean's cheeks warmed again. "I may have watched it a few dozen times. I'm not that observant in real life," Jean grinned sheepishly. "If I could replay scenes from real life, maybe I wouldn't be so socially awkward."

"You don't seem socially awkward to me, but I am curious how you'd replay the 'scene' of meeting me if you had the chance." Christina's smile turned impish.

Would I be more direct and confident if I could do this weekend over again? Could I have made this connection happen last night?

Before Jean could answer, Harmony—of all people—came bouncing up to the table.

"Hey, Christina! I've been looking for you!" she said, bursting into the conversation with that bubbling confidence Jean found both enviable and obnoxious.

"You have?" Christina stood, eyebrows raised.

"Yeah, they want you backstage to prep for the costume contest," Harmony said. She didn't spare Jean so much as a sideways glance.

"Already?" Christina asked.

"Yup. The masquerade is one of the most popular events, so everybody needs to get mic-ed up and all, I guess," Harmony explained with a shrug. "I don't know all the details; I'm just 'go-fer' with a simple directive: bring you over to the mainstage."

"Oh, okay," Christina agreed. She turned to Jean, touched her arm, and gave her a sweet smile. "Hope to see you there, *Francesca*," she said with a tiny wave of her fingers.

Jean's heart swelled, and she nodded rapidly. Now Harmony did look at Jean. Her smile dropped for a split second, just long enough for Jean to catch a glimpse of hostility. *She really hates me now.* Jean didn't know why she cared, but it still stung.

"Come, m'lady," Harmony looped her arm through Christina's, and Jean watched as the two walked off together, chummy as a pair of old friends. *When Christina looks at Harmony, she sees Harmony. When she looks at me, does she see* me *at all, or am I just a surrogate for Lindsey?* Jean smoothed the sides of her dress. *Does it matter? If it's a way in, it's a way in. Right?*

Chapter 13:
Harmony

Harmony was honestly surprised when Christina so readily accepted her arm. It was a thrilling development in the relationship Harmony was trying to build with the actress. Harmony had been worried when she found Christina with Jean. Their conversation looked so *intimate*.

Jean had been wearing a new High School Bites costume. It was another perfect replica; darkly gothic and jaw-droppingly sexy. The deep wine red dress had a plunging neckline that reached her sternum; it had immediately drawn Harmony's attention straight to Jean's chest. It had taken serious concentration not to stare at her small, perky boobs. *Forget about Jean's boobs,* Harmony lectured herself as she led Christina through the convention.

"Wasn't her dress *fantastic*?" Christina cooed as they walked.

"Yeah, it was pretty." Harmony didn't want to talk about Jean, but Christina seemed to *really* like that cosplay because she wouldn't shut up about it the entire way to the mainstage.

"It's going to be hard to be an impartial judge with such a perfect Francesa in the mix," Christina said with a grin.

"Just wait, there are some incredibly impressive cosplays this year," Harmony replied, trying to steer the conversation away from *Jean*. "I saw a *killer* Thanos earlier today."

"Who's Thanos?" Christina asked. Harmony tried not to balk openly.

"Thanos, you know, from the Marvel universe," Harmony said.

"Sorry, I've never gotten around to watching those movies," Christina said.

Seriously? None of them? Harmony remembered how Jean had lectured her on 'gatekeeping' and kept her shock to herself.

"I don't watch a lot of movies," Christina went on. "I pretty much only watch them when I'm flying."

"What kind of movies?" Harmony asked.

"Stupid comedies mostly." Christina waved her hand. "Flying is too stressful for serious stuff."

"I can understand that logic," Harmony agreed. She stopped in front of the small back door to the auditorium where the masquerade would be held. "Well, here we are. Good luck, and have fun." Harmony gave Christina a quick hug, which Christina returned.

"Thank you, Harmony," she said. "I'll see you around the parties tonight, right?"

"Absolutely!" Harmony confirmed. When the door shut behind Christina, Harmony meandered back through the hotel until she came across a gaggle of familiar faces.

"Hey, Harmony!" Chris waved her over. "We were going to go to a restaurant for an early dinner."

"Early dinner?" Harmony looked at her watch. "More like a late lunch."

"I disagree. I think the distinction hinges less on time and more on intent and circumstance," Chris countered.

"What circumstance makes eating at midafternoon early dinner rather than late lunch?" Harmony raised an eyebrow.

"Having already eaten lunch," Chris explained.

"Then just call it second lunch," offered Gabby.

"There is no second lunch; there's only second *breakfast*," said Chris, slipping into a British accent in imitation of Pippin.

"I object to that rule; I eat second dinner all the time," Gabby said, raising a finger.

"Why can't you call your lunch second breakfast and make this lunch?" Harmony asked Chris.

"Because I don't eat hotdogs for breakfast," Chris said, sticking his tongue out at Harmony.

"Elevensies?" Jeff offered.

"This argument is getting ridiculous," Ginny chimed in.

"*Getting*? It was ridiculous from the out," Gabby said with a laugh. "Can we just call it 'linner' and go get some food?" She looked at Harmony and Chris with raised eyebrows.

"I suppose we don't have to agree on the semantics of the meal to eat it together," Harmony conceded.

"Okay," agreed Chris. "But I'm sticking with early dinner because I do not intend to eat another meal today."

"If you use that logic, do all meal names become meaningless if you don't have three meals a day?" Jeff asked as the group began to walk out the door.

"What? No, that's absurd," said Harmony with a shake of her head.

"If you have only two meals, are they then brunch and linner?" Ginny asked.

"That is also absurd," Harmony replied, pointing a finger at Ginny.

"This whole conversation is absurd," Gabby rightly pointed out.

"What did you expect? You're at JanCon," Chris said, and Harmony laughed in agreement. It was about par for the course as conversations with this bunch tended to be. Outside, on the sidewalk, they were joined by Kaolin. The six of them walked two-by-two down the street toward a bar and restaurant that served basic American fare.

"Hey, Kaolin," Harmony said as they walked. "I haven't seen you in the game room playing Zar, so I wasn't even sure you were here."

"One does not, in fact, need to be *in* the game room to play Zar," Kaolin laughed.

"Fair point," Harmony conceded.

"Hey, Kaolin, you should play this Jean chick. She wiped the floor with us last night; she might give you a run for your money," Chris said.

Harmony bristled. Did Jean have to pop up *everywhere* at con? Even in conversation with her friends? "There's a lot of *luck* involved in Zar. She wasn't that special," Harmony said with a pout.

"Oh, but skill does play a significant role," Kaolin insisted.

"Are you going to WorldCon again this year?" Harmony asked, abruptly changing the subject to something else she knew would generate conversation. She was considering going to WorldCon at some point, and she enjoyed hearing people talk about it.

The rest of dinner, or linner or whatever it was, went by without any mention of Jean. They got seated quickly because of the odd hour, which Harmony appreciated. She made a mental note for next year. She treated herself to steak and mashed potatoes and had a pleasant time. The true reason for the early dinner didn't become apparent until they were all back at the hotel. Ginny and Chris wanted to be back in time to get good seats for the masquerade.

"Don't you want to go?" Gabby asked Harmony when she didn't follow the others toward the auditorium.

"No," Harmony replied.

"Are you sure?" Gabby asked, taking out her program and flipping through the schedule. "There's not a lot else going on, and if there's a chance you'll want to go, there isn't much time to decide. We should get in line soon if we want decent seats or seats at all. With Christina as one of the judges, I'm sure it'll be packed."

Harmony wrinkled her nose. Go to the masquerade, just so she could watch from the audience as Christina fawned over Jean in her maddeningly sexy costume, showing off her perfect looks? Sit and watch that while also knowing Jean is a dyed-in-the-wool geek, born and raised in fandom, probably crazy smart, and perfect for Christina in every way Harmony was and wasn't? No thanks.

"I'm up for pretty much anything *other* than that," Harmony grumped.

"How about karaoke?" Gabby suggested.

"Okay, but we have to hit the bar first."

"You need to get drunk before you sing?" Gabby asked with a smirk.

"Yes, but more than that, I gotta make sure the audience is drunk before I sing, including you." Harmony pushed Gabby in the direction of the consuite. "Come on, let's go."

Harmony tried, but she just couldn't get as tipsy as she would have liked before Gabby pushed her up onto the karaoke stage. Harmony stepped up to the mic. She felt her heart pounding in her chest and the adrenalin in her veins making her hands shake. She grinned at the "audience"—a dozen geeks sitting around a hotel room watching her.

"Hi, my name is Harmony. Yes, that's my real name, and in a few seconds, you're going to find out how ironic it is." Harmony smiled as her joke got a couple laughs. The music started up, and Harmony began to belt out the lyrics to *Mr. Blue Sky*. By the end of the song, a combination of the adrenaline and con punch had Harmony in a bright, outgoing mood. She immediately signed up for several more slots before sitting down beside Gabby to wait for her turn to come around again.

"Whew, that was fun!" Harmony grinned and wiped sweat from her forehead.

"You did good, *Harmony*, but maybe you should bring Melody along to sing with you next time; you could use some help with yours," Gabby teased.

"Ha!" Harmony laughed. "For that, you're coming up there with me for the next one."

"What are we singing?" Gabby asked.

"Hooked on a Feeling," Harmony said with a grin, wondering if her friend would get the connection.

Gabby gave her a lop-sided grin. "You're doing a Guardians of the Galaxy theme?"

Of course, she got it. Harmony nodded an enthusiastic affirmation. The soundtracks had been running through her head ever since her conversation with Christina. "You know, it's kind of ridiculous to have Christina judge a costume contest if she isn't going to get so many of the references," Harmony said, thinking out loud.

"Why wouldn't she get the references?" Gabby asked.

"She's never seen any of the Avengers movies; she didn't even know who Thanos was!" Harmony scoffed. It didn't *bother* her really—it's not as if Harmony would be going out to the movies with Christina—it just seemed illogical and unfair to those in the contest *not* doing High School Bites cosplays.

"Maybe she's just a DC girl," Gabby suggested.

"No, it's the whole genre. And even if she were," Harmony stuck out her tongue. "Boo, DC. Marvel rules."

"I didn't realize you hated DC," said Gabby.

"I'm not saying I *hate* it, just that it's inferior," she stated as fact.

"So let me get this straight," Gabby tilted her head. "You're saying you didn't want to go to the masquerade because you don't respect Christina as a judge because she doesn't watch Marvel movies? That doesn't sound like you."

"No," Harmony admitted. She chewed the inside of her cheek, thinking. *If I can't tell Gabby, who can I tell?* She sighed. "It's because of that stupid pretty cosplayer, *Jean*. Christina is all over her, and it's hard to watch when I want her all over *me*."

"So, you're into the cosplayer?" Gabby asked.

"What? No! I'm into Christina, duh." Harmony rolled her eyes. It was a ridiculous assertion; Harmony had been talking about nothing but Christina all con long.

"You sure about that?" Gabby asked, squinting accusingly at her.

Harmony's guts did a little twist. *Am I?* Harmony looked away. "Oh, hey, it's our turn to sing." Harmony grabbed Gabby and dragged her to the mic, chanting, *"Ooga chaka, ooga, ooga, ooga chaka..."*

Chapter 14:
Jean

Saturday, 9:15pm

Jean didn't win the costume contest. As flattering as the judges' comments were—and Christina's were quite complimentary—she could tell from the off that they were going to vote for the large General Grievous with his four independently moving arms and glowing lightsabers. Jean didn't want to be disappointed, but she was. And the disappointment fed the general disquiet that had been growing in her chest since her conversation with Christina.

Putting on a costume and adopting the persona of a character had always helped Jean boost her confidence. Being Francesca made her feel brave and sexy, and Christina seemed to be responding to that. But that wasn't *her*, it wasn't *Jean*. At best, the person flirting with Christina was some Jean-Francesca-Lindsey hybrid. The whole thing left Jean wondering if she was capable of navigating the convention and her interactions with Christina as herself.

When the contest was over, and the crowd dispersed, Jean went back to her room. She opened her suitcase and stared at its contents. She hadn't packed for a social version of herself. She had a few mundane clothing items to wear to and from the convention, her costumes, and her comfy but frumpy gray sweats—the outfit she'd been wearing when she flounced out of the game room like a pouting child. And she had the new corset she'd bought yesterday.

Can I put together these pieces into something that is me and not Francesca? Jean lifted up the corset. *Yes. I can. And if Christina can be interested in me as me, then maybe we really could get together, if only for tonight.*

Jean left her room an hour later dressed in the black lycra shorts she'd worn under her Francesca dress, the tall boots from Friday's costume, and her new black silk corset. She'd taken out her fangs—the thought of kissing while wearing them had lost its allure—and redone her makeup to look more natural. Jean didn't often dress this way—it was nowhere near her day-to-day look—but she was herself; she was Jean, not Francesca. The outfit helped her call on the most confident parts of her authentic self. Jean looked at her reflection. *I'm still me, just the "party time" version.* She felt good about that.

Jean took a deep breath—or as deep as the corset allowed—and stepped out of the elevator onto the main party room floor. The hallway was moderately crowded and buzzing with a mix of voices and music. Jean wandered from room to room, sampling each party. It was early yet, so although the parties were busy, they weren't as rowdy as they would be by night's end. There were familiar themes: pirates, Star Trek, zombies, even an adorable little Hobbit hole offering some hoppy home-brewed ale that Jean choked down while chatting with the man who had made it. He was very proud of his beer, and Jean was sure that some people would find it fantastic. Still, the second she was done, she gobbled down several pieces of "lembas bread"—which were basically large triangle-shaped shortbread cookies— until the bitter taste left her mouth.

I can't overeat; this corset is not that forgiving. Nearly every party offered refreshments in keeping with their themes. And many of those refreshments included alcohol. The pirate grog was exceptionally tasty, and Jean had two cups as she talked costuming with Nellie, a woman in an impressive Klingon costume.

"Why didn't you enter the costume contest?" Jean asked, marveling at the exquisite hand-made details of her cosplay while trying not to stare at the woman's ample cleavage.

"That thing is so political," Nellie scoffed. "Klingons never win anyhow. We're too old school."

Jean nodded agreeably. As much as she tried to stay focused on the people around her, she always had one eye out for Christina. Whenever she caught a glimpse of a blonde-haired woman, she did a double-take.

Jean's eyes were scanning the crowds in the hallways when she caught sight of a different familiar face.*Harmony*. Jean gritted her teeth. Small cons could be a little *too* small sometimes. Harmony was standing at the end of the hall, drink in hand, chatting with another woman while that nitwit Jeff hovered nearby. Harmony had changed her clothes for the parties too; she wore jeans and a tight-fitting purple tank top that blatantly showed off her large chest. Jeff was not-so-subtly gawking at her ample bosom while Harmony talked. *Is she wearing makeup?* Something about Harmony's face looked fresher—somehow even cuter than before.

Jean frowned. *She's looking for Christina too*, she thought bitterly. *And if Christina is a boob girl...* Jean glanced down at her own small chest, propped up by the corset for maximum cleavage. Her maximum wasn't all that much. She sighed. *It's fine. I look good.* She ran her hands along the curved sides of the corset. When she looked back up, Harmony was looking at her. Quickly Jean ducked into the closest party room. She preferred the company of just about anybody besides Harmony. Although she was still hopeful that she'd find the one person she wanted to talk to most of all. *Where is Christina?*

Chapter 15:
Harmony

The first thing that Harmony noticed when she caught sight of Jean in the hallway of the party floor was that Jean was wearing the *exact* corset that Gabby had been planning to buy. They had gone back to the dealers' room later that night only to find the coveted corset had already been purchased. Gabby had missed out on something she wanted because of the stupid fire alarm, and Jean had scooped in and taken it away. *She gets in the way of just about everything,* Harmony thought, trying not to scowl.

Jean did pull it off quite well, Harmony hated to admit it, but it was true. The black corset contrasted with Jean's pale skin and drew attention to her small round breasts, making Harmony's mouth water and her chest ache with envy. *My boobs would look far too big in that.* Jean's breasts were so obnoxiously perfect. Harmony could easily imagine Christina's hand cupping them, caressing that lovely handful. *Cut it out,* Harmony snapped at herself inside her mind. Although the mental picture of Christina fondling Jean was hot as hell, it also created sharp painful shards of jealousy that cut her up inside.

"What are you staring at?" Gabby asked. She turned her head to look. "Her again? Why are you so obsessed with her?"

Jean disappeared into a party room, and Harmony grabbed Gabby by the elbow, dragging her away from Jeff in the opposite direction of Jean.

"I'm not *obsessed* with her," Harmony protested. "Like I said, I just don't like how chummy she's getting with Christina. She's the competition, and I don't like to lose."

"I don't know; it seems more and more like you might like her," Gabby pulled her arm from Harmony's grasp and elbowed her in the ribs.

"Like hell, I do," Harmony said a little too forcefully; she felt her cheeks warm. "I like Christina, okay?" she added in what she hoped was a less defensive tone.

"Yeah, yeah, yeah, she's your Everest. I get it. But say you do get Christina, what happens after you 'mount' her?" Gabby asked without pausing for

Harmony to respond. "Nothing. She moves on to the next city and the next convention."

"And the next fan," Harmony finished. "I know. I'm not looking for the love of my life. I mean, that would be cool, miraculous even. But I'd settle for having sex with my dream girl. Hell, I'd be excited to get a kiss at this point."

"But if you hooked up with the cutie you keep staring at—another fan like you—who knows, it might have the potential to actually go somewhere," Gabby pointed out with infuriatingly sound logic.

"I doubt it. Cosplayers aren't usually my type," Harmony said dismissively.

Gabby raised an eyebrow. "And actresses are? Aren't they just basically professional cosplayers?"

"What? No, they aren't," Harmony scoffed. And you were talking about a *relationship,* and I already told you I'm not looking for a relationship from Christina."

"How is acting not like professional cosplaying?" Gabby asked, pressing the point.

"Cosplay is about making the costume," Harmony reasoned.

"Not for all cosplayers," Gabby said. When Harmony did nothing more than stare back at her,

Gabby raised a teasing eyebrow. "Hashtag not all cosplayers?" she joked, tapping the middle and index fingers of her two hands together.

"I'm ignoring you now." Harmony turned away.

"Well, do whatever you want. It's getting too crowded up here." Gabby fanned her face with her pocket program. "I'm going to go down to the gaming area."

"Okay, I'm going to see if I can't find Christina in one of these party rooms," Harmony replied, and the two parted ways. Harmony skipped the first two rooms in an attempt to avoid running into Jean again. *Why did Gabby have to say that about liking her?* The comment had only served to intensify the uneasy feeling in Harmony's gut when she thought of the woman.

Harmony stepped into the next room and immediately spotted Christina, sitting on a bed, chatting with several men. She looked relaxed and casual, leaning back on one arm, a drink in the other. She'd changed into black leggings and a loose-fitting, sleeveless blouse with a plunging neckline decorated with shining black rhinestones. Christina's fair cheeks were flushed, whether from the heat of the room or the drink in her hand Harmony didn't know. She felt her own cheeks burn when Christina caught her eye and smiled familiarly at her. The men flanking Christina continued to talk to her, but Christina kept her face turned towards Harmony, a faint smile on her lips as if silently inviting her to interrupt the conversation. Harmony was more than happy to oblige.

Harmony squeezed past one of the men and climbed onto the bed. She bounced a little as she settled herself near the headrest, crossing her legs kindergarten-style. Christina twisted toward Harmony and away from the two men.

"Harmony, it's good to see you again. I've been meaning to ask you something." Christina turned back to the men. "Excuse me," she said politely.

"Oh, go ahead," one of the men responded but didn't move or look away. When it became clear that neither man intended to abandon their seats next to the actress, Christina slipped off her shoes and climbed fully onto the bed. She put her back to the two clueless dudes and faced Harmony, pulling her feet up beside herself.

"Hello there," Harmony chirped. "I'm glad I caught up with you."

"Me too," Christina glanced sideways rolled her eyes toward the men behind her. "*So* glad." It was clear as day what Christina was really saying. *Thank you for saving me from those guys.* Harmony was only glad to help. It was thrilling to be with her tv crush in such an informal setting—sitting on a bed together in their socks. Christina was wearing blue wool socks, and Harmony had on her very favorite *SpongeBob* pair. Harmony pulled on her feet and rocked a bit, trying to contain her fangirl glee.

"How is life on the convention circuit?" Harmony asked.

"It's good. I really *do* like meeting fans," Christina's eyes sparkled. *Fans like you*, they said.

"Does it get monotonous? All the travel and signings and questions and constant attention from your *adoring* fans?" Harmony asked.

"The signing does get to be a little much—like I said before. It's repetitious; I swear I think my hand does it in my sleep sometimes." Christina lifted her hand and mimed signing her autograph. Her finger traced the letters of her name in the air. *Christina Darlington.* She sighed and dropped her hand back to the bed.

"Yeah, I can imagine," said Harmony.

"But the rest, no. I wouldn't call it monotonous," Christina continued. "Every convention is different, and I'm visiting a lot of places I'd never been to before."

"How's JanCon treating you?" Harmony gestured to the room around them.

"I'm enjoying myself," Christina answered, nodding. "Although I do miss home sometimes," she added.

"Do you have a girlfriend back home you're missing?" Harmony asked, hoping her tone adequately conveyed her flirtatious meaning.

"No, just my pets," Christina pressed her lips together as if suppressing a smile.

Harmony grinned. She shifted in bed so that her position mirrored Christina's. "What kind of pets do you have?" Harmony lightly brushed her fingers against Christina's as she asked. Christina moved her index finger and ever so slightly stroked Harmony's hand in response. The simple touch made goosebumps rush up the back of Harmony's neck.

"I have a cat named Rufus and a dog named Bubba," Christina began to fondly talk about her pets as they both slowly and subtly allowed their hands to come closer together. Harmony tried to listen through the sound of her heartbeat thumping in her ears. *We're flirting; we're touching. This actually might happen.* Harmony's stomach fluttered, her mind spinning like a pinwheel in the wind.

The sight of Jean entering the room behind Christina suddenly caught Harmony's attention. She met Jean's eye, and the cosplayer looked away. *Freaking Jean.* Harmony mentally shook herself off. *Ignore her. Christina is talking; pay attention.* Harmony refocused her concentration on Christina.

"What about you?" Christina asked, batting her long lashes, her crystal blue eyes fixed on Harmony's face.

"Me? Oh," Harmony froze. *What were we talking about? Pets, right.* "I don't have any pets, although my *completely platonic* roommate and I have talked about getting a lizard."

"A lizard?" Christina shuddered theatrically.

"Not a fan of reptiles?" Harmony asked with a light laugh.

Christina shook her head violently, sending her long blonde hair flying around her face. "No way. I like things that are soft and cuddly," she said.

Now that's a perfect opening if I've ever heard one. "I'm soft and cuddly," Harmony said. She reached out and tucked Christina's hair behind one ear. "Do you like me?"

Some random lady chose that moment to barge into the conversation, dropping down into the chair next to the bed and tapping Christina eagerly on the shoulder. With an apologetic shrug, Christina turned to the woman and greeted her with bright, false cheer as the woman began to speak rapidly at the actress. Harmony pursed her lips in a pout Christina didn't see. *What now?*

Across the room, Harmony caught sight of Jean once again. She was standing alone in the far corner, sipping a drink and watching her. *No, she's not looking at me; she's looking at Christina.* Harmony studied Jean's unreadable features. *Seriously, why does she seem to show up everywhere? Conversely, why do I always notice her?*

"Harmony?" Christina's arm on her shoulder brought Harmony back to herself and the beautiful actress sitting beside her.

"Have you met Betsy here?" Christina asked. "She told me she was interested in getting more involved with conventions. I thought you two could chat." Christina's eyes held Harmony's; she tilted her head slightly. '*Help me out, please?*' her expression said.

"No, I haven't. I'd love to talk to you about it," Harmony piped. Sitting up and leaning over Christina's shoulder, she whispered, "Find me later?" She covertly slipped her room key into Christina's hand.

"Thank you," Christina whispered back, her breath hot against Harmony's cheek. Inside, Harmony was doing cartwheels, while on the outside, she calmly watched as Christina excused herself and slipped out of the room.

"So you want to get involved in the convention?" Harmony turned her attention to Betsy. Betsy excitedly began to tell Harmony about how wonderful her con-going experience had been so far and all the ways she thought she could be of use. When she could get a word in edgewise, Harmony explained to Besty how volunteering was organized and strongly encouraged her to visit the volunteer table.

The next time Harmony looked up, Jean was no longer in the room. She glanced at her watch. It was getting late. *What if Christina actually comes to my room? I should probably get back there…*

Chapter 16: Jean

Jean was on her second round of the party circuit when she found Christina and Harmony sitting together on a hotel room bed. They were in the middle of a crowded but relatively tame party, but the way Harmony looked at Christina, you would think they were alone in that bedroom.

Jean quickly averted her gaze, moving along the edge of the room until she reached the refreshment table. She'd had quite enough to eat *and* drink that night. But she couldn't very well just turn and go now—it would feel too awkward.

Jean straightened her back within her corset and tried to find space for even one more bite. She looked at the table. Cake. There was no way she had room for cake. A man with a curling mustache and slight frame stood behind the table, grinning at her.

"Can I get you some cake? Or maybe a drink?" he offered.

"A drink, yes, thank you." Jean ran her hand over the corset. "No room left for cake, I'm afraid."

"Say no more," the man lifted a hand. "I've worn a corset or two in my day. A drink it is."

"Thank you." Jean nodded at him as she took her drink. She took a sip. *Yikes!* It was far too strong to drink quickly. *Sipping slowly is probably a better choice anyhow.* Jean found a spot along the wall and risked another glance in Christina's direction. It was hard to see much of Christina from her vantage point at the edge of the room, but Harmony was in plain sight. The way she sat, lounging on the bed, oozed sex and made her cleavage impossible to ignore. *Christina can probably see right down Harmony's shirt,* Jean mused. That was the point, after all, she assumed. Harmony was coming on strong to Christina tonight. No more bouncing cheerfulness; her expression was all seduction. The term 'bedroom eyes' came to mind.

Harmony's head turned slightly, her gaze falling on Jean. *Shit.* Jean immediately looked away and tried to act as if she didn't notice Harmony glaring at her as if Jean were some unwanted vermin. Jean stood stock-still until Harmony looked away. She let out a breath and felt the corset shift around her ribcage. *I should loosen this thing.*

Jean had tied it herself—it had been no small feat. The front of the corset clipped together with metal busks, but the back was laced from her shoulder blades down to the small of her back. If adjusted correctly, even a tight corset could be worn comfortably for hours, but Jean's was proving to be a touch too snug toward the bottom and loose at the top.

Across the room, Christina stood and walked toward the door. *Should I follow her?* Jean's insides twinged. She knew she was getting a side-stitch and needed to fix her corset. It would be easy enough for somebody else to adjust if they knew what they were doing. *Didn't the guy who made my drink say he had experience with corsets?*

"Excuse me," Jean approached the mustachioed man. "This might be an odd thing to ask, but could you help me adjust the laces of my corset? It's too tight here and loose here," Jean explained, pointing.

"Of course I can help with that," he quickly agreed. "Let's step into the hall, and I'll see what I can do."

Jean followed him out of the room. The hallway felt cool and breezy after being in the stuffy room. She tried to guide her helper in how to alleviate the problem, although he struggled to follow her instruction. Jean stared at her feet as he yanked the strings this way and that. She was about to tell him to give up when a high soft voice whispered in Jean's ear.

"Here, let me help you with that."

"Huh?" Jean turned her head. Christina was standing just behind her shoulder. Before Jean could gather her wits enough to speak, Christina had taken the man's place and was gently pulling at her corset lacing.

"There," she said. "Feel better?"

"Oh, yes, thank you," Jean said breathlessly. Christina hadn't just adjusted the laces but had loosened them considerably. *Why would she do that?*

"That bodice looks wonderful on you." Christina leaned close until her lips brushed Jean's ear. "But it would look even better on my floor," she added in a throaty whisper. A shiver ran down Jean's spine, and goosebumps broke out across her skin. *Oh my.* Jean's breath caught in her throat. She didn't know how to respond. *She is coming on to me as me this time for sure, right?* Christina lightly ran her fingers down Jean's arm, and Jean shivered again. *Does it matter?*

"Christina, I—"

"Shhh," Christina hushed her as she pressed something flat and rectangular into Jean's hand. *A card?* Christina's breath was hot on Jean's skin as she planted a soft kiss at the nape of Jean's neck. "I'll give you a minute to think about it." Christina kissed her again, and Jean closed her eyes, her fingers tightening around the object in her hand. Christina stepped back, and Jean looked down her hand. *Christina's room key?* Jean turned, shocked, to stare at the actress.

"I hope I see you soon, *Francesca*." Christina winked, turned on her heel, and sauntered off while Jean stared dumbly after her. *Did that really just happen?* Jean looked again at the key; she slid it out of its little paper sleeve. Yes, it was a keycard for a room at this hotel. *But which room?* Jean slid it back into the sleeve and turned it over in her hand. On the back, handwritten in black sharpie, was a number.

Holy shit. Christina Darlington just invited me back to her room. Jean leaned against the wall to keep from falling over. She put a hand on her stomach; she couldn't blame the corset for her lack of breath this time. Jean ran her fingers along the smooth silk fabric. '*It would look even better on my floor.*' Christina's voice echoed in her head.

Do I do it? Do I go to her room? Jean closed her eyes, and butterflies of excitement and uncertainty fluttered in her chest. *She's the girl I've been in love with since I was a teen. Why wouldn't I go?* Jean rolled her head against the wall, wondering what was stopping her. 'I hope to see you soon, Francesca.' Jean sighed. That was it, wasn't it? Christina didn't want Jean. *But do I really want Christina? It was her character Alessia that I'd fallen in love with, after all.* Jean looked down at the key in her hand. *Does it matter?*

Chapter 17:
Harmony

Saturday, 11:33pm

Harmony chewed on the inside of her cheek as she debated her options. If she went back to her room now and Christina never showed, she would miss out on socializing and gaming at the convention for nothing. But if Christina did show up and Harmony wasn't there, she'd hate herself forever for missing out on the chance to hook up with her first girl-crush. She carefully weighed the odds and trade-offs, measuring the level of emotional response she felt at each possible outcome. In the end, hope won out, and Harmony hopped off the bed. Leaving the parties and friends behind, she caught an elevator up to her room.

"Well, shit," Harmony said aloud when she opened the door. She'd forgotten what a *mess* she always made of her hotel rooms. There was old food on the dresser, clothes scattered on the bed, a wet towel on the bathroom floor. *I hope she doesn't show up too soon,*

Harmony thought as she hastily began to tidy up the room.

She was overheated and sweaty by the time she was done. She sniffed her armpits. Not great. *If I take a shower, and she shows up while I'm in there, that could actually be pretty hot.* Harmony stripped off her dirty clothes and put them away. She turned the shower faucet until the water was scorching hot. She left the door to the bathroom open as she showered, listening for the sound of a card key in the lock, but none came.

Cleaned to her satisfaction, Harmony turned off the water and began to towel dry. She took extra care to scrunch her curls so that they would hang in ringlets. She looked at herself in the full-length mirror next to the hotel room closet. Her skin looked fresh and pink from the hot water. She appreciated the aesthetic of her smoothly shaved legs and labia. The cool air of the room made her nipples harden. Harmony lightly pinched one nipple and sighed as the touch sent a tiny shiver of pleasure across her bare skin. She smiled at her reflection. *I look pretty hot naked.*

Harmony wondered if being naked when Christina showed up would be too forward. *Probably.* She dug through her bag for the red lace bra and cheeky red panties she'd brought for just such an occasion. She added a touch of makeup—just mascara and lip gloss— and checked herself out in the mirror once more. *Damn, I look good. I hope all this sexiness doesn't go to waste. If Christina doesn't show up, I could always text Chris for a booty call.* She would much rather see Christina; she had been in the mood for *female* companionship. But she looked so hot she'd turned herself on. Harmony ran her hands along her waist and shifted her hips side to side. She could feel the warmth of arousal between her thighs. She was tempted to touch herself. *Wait, not yet. Enjoy the anticipation.*

Harmony dimmed the lights in the room as she waited. Time ticked by. Harmony fiddled with her phone. *How long should I wait?* Just when she thought the anticipation might actually kill her, Harmony's ears caught the sound of footsteps in the hallway. They were moving in her direction. Harmony strained to hear while resisting the urge to press her ear to the door. The footsteps stopped. *She's outside my room.* Harmony's heart began to race. She stepped around the corner and lay herself down on the bed in what she hoped was a sexy pose. The lock beeped, and she heard the door slowly open.

"Come in," Harmony called out in a sweet, singsong voice. The door closed, and Harmony held her breath. *I can't believe this is actually happening.*

Chapter 18:
Jean

Saturday, 11:50pm

Jean barely remembered the journey from the party floor to Christina's room, but before she knew it, there she was, standing outside a hotel room door, trying not to hyperventilate at the thought of what waited for her on the other side of that door: a dream come true. It would be the fulfillment of a long-held fantasy or its destruction. With a shaking hand, Jean slid the key into the lock. She held her breath as she slowly opened the door and stepped into the dimly lit room.

"Come in," a voice called, and Jean let the door shut behind her. Something about that voice wasn't quite right. *You're just nervous*, she told herself.

Jean stepped further into the room, past the bathroom, until she could see the bed. Jean stopped dead. The woman draped seductively across the mattress in bright red lingerie wasn't Christina.

"H-Harmony?" Jean balked.

Harmony jumped and nearly fell off the bed. Jean watched, frozen in place as Harmony got awkwardly to her feet. "Jean? What are you doing here?"

"I thought this was Christina's…"

Harmony tilted her head. "Why would you think that?"

"I, uh, Christina gave me her room key…" Jean sputtered as her brain scrambled to make sense of the situation.

"Only, this is my room," Harmony said, eyes narrowing. "Meaning, Christina gave you *my* room key."

"How did she…? Why did she have…?" Jean didn't seem to be capable of finishing an entire sentence in her state of shock.

"I gave her my key," Harmony said. "She must have mixed them up." She ran a hand across her face, then looked at Jean and grinned. "Well, this is awkward, huh?"

Awkward didn't begin to cover it. This wasn't just any mix-up. Somehow instead of ending up with the woman of her dreams, Jean was standing in the room of her competition—the bubbling, beautiful woman who kept showing up everywhere had shown up again *in her underwear*.

"You, of all people." Jean shook her head.

"What do you mean 'of all people?'" Harmony put a hand on her hip, apparently unbothered by her state of undress, and pursed her lips. "It's not like I did this on purpose."

"I didn't say that you did." Jean crossed her arms and glared right back at Harmony.

"Then why are you acting like you're mad at *me*? Me 'of all people', as you say. I haven't done anything," Harmony protested.

"You hate me," Jean stated.

Harmony scoffed. "What? I do not."

Jean rolled her eyes. "Please." She snorted. "You've treated me like unwanted vermin all weekend."

"Have not," Harmony said with a little pouty whine to her voice.

"Seriously? Can you honestly say you haven't been colder with me than with pretty much everybody else here?" Jean challenged her.

Harmony dropped her hand from her hip, her expression morphing from defiance to unwilling contrition. "Fine. I guess I haven't been my most friendly self to you." Harmony reluctantly agreed, her chest sagging with the admission. "But I haven't really meant to. It was mostly subconscious." Harmony pursed her lips again and looked appraisingly at Jean. She straightened her shoulders. "There's a perfectly simple reason, you know."

"What do you mean?" Jean asked. What "simple reason" could Harmony have to act with such hostility? Jean had never done anything to deserve it.

"Isn't it obvious? You were my rival for Christina," said Harmony. "And you're tough competition. I don't like to lose."

Jean opened her mouth, but she didn't know what to say.

"But I don't hate you," Harmony added. "I'm just jealous and insecure."

Jean shook her head in disbelief. "Insecure? You?" She scoffed. Harmony was the very definition of confidence. She hopped around JanCon like she could fit in anywhere, befriend anyone. *Anyone but me.* "Why would *I* make you jealous?" Jean asked, indignant. "You know everybody here; you can talk to anybody—"

"And you're fucking *gorgeous*!" Harmony exclaimed. "You're just so..." She gestured at Jean.

"Everything about you is *perfect*. How could I stand a chance against you?" Harmony's mouth turned down, a longing sadness passing over her face. "Sure, I can walk up and talk to Christina. But she *wants* to talk to you."

The room went quiet for a moment as Jean considered Harmony's assertation. It was true that Christina had approached *her* tonight, not Harmony; she'd given Jean the room key, not the other way around. If it had been a contest, she had won. *But Christina didn't want me*; she *wanted Lindsey.* "She only liked me because I look like Francesca," Jean said softly. "I'm just a cosplay doll. Nothing more."

"That's not true," Harmony said firmly. "You're so much more, and anybody who spends two minutes talking with you would see that. Sure, maybe you caught her eye with your costume, but come on. You're the total package: smart, geeky, and magnitudes better looking than anyone else here. Of course, she'd want *you.*"

Jean took a moment to really look at Harmony. The woman exuded a sexy confidence that filled the room like a strong perfume. She was a vision. The contour of her hourglass figure, which dipped in at her waist and curved softly out to her hips, was goddess-like in its perfection. She looked into Harmony's wide, expressive eyes.

"I can't believe for a minute that you don't know how sexy you are," Jean said.

Harmony blinked at her. "You think I'm sexy?"

"You're incredibly sexy. I mean, God, just look at you." Jean looked again down the length of Harmony's body—at the lingerie that cupped her voluptuous breasts and hid the sweet treasure between her legs. Jean felt a twinge between her own legs, and she knew that looking at Harmony was turning her on. *Shit. I like her.* Jean's face burned as she forced her eyes back up to meet Harmony's. *I really like her.* Harmony looked quizzically back. *I'm an idiot*, Jean thought, her chest tingling with some combination of attraction and embarrassment. *What am I doing standing here staring at her?* Jean turned toward the door. "I'm sorry," she stammered, "I should probably go—"

"Wait," Harmony stopped her before she could take another step. Jean's pulse was rushing in her ears as Harmony took her hand and turned her back around. "Show me," Harmony whispered.

"What?"

"Don't leave. Stay." Harmony leaned toward Jean. "Show me."

"What?" Jean repeated.

"Show me that you think I'm hot. Show me, and I'll show you that I really don't hate you." Harmony's voice was soft and breathless. She stopped; her lips were so close to Jean's that Jean could almost feel them. Before she knew what she was doing, Jean closed the gap and pressed her lips to Harmony's. They were so soft and warm. She buried her fingers in Harmony's curls and pulled her closer, their kiss deepening. Jean let her tongue venture out, and it was met enthusiastically by Harmony's. Jean felt a flickering burn inside her chest and a warm throbbing between her legs. She kissed Harmony faster, unable to get enough of the sensation, of the dance that their tongues were doing. Harmony's touch had sparked a firestorm of desire within Jean.

"I want you," she whispered against Harmony's lips.

"Good," Harmony breathed. "Because I really want you too."

Harmony's fingers traced up the center of Jean's corset; when her fingers found the top hook, she pulled back and looked questioningly at Jean. Jean nodded, and

Harmony began to unclasp the bodice, her eyes on her work until each clasp was undone. The corset fell to the floor. Jean shivered as her bare nipples responded to the cool air and her own arousal.

Harmony sighed, her hand moving to cup one small breast. Jean moaned encouragingly and kissed Harmony again. As their mouths hungrily devoured one another, Harmony softly kneaded Jean's breast with one hand while the other wrapped around her waist, pulling her close.

"Oh God," Jean breathed as Harmony pinched her nipple. Jean felt a tingling warmth spread within her until she knew her panties were probably soaking wet. Jean tugged at Harmony, leading her, stumbling to the bed, pausing only long enough to peel off her shorts before dropping onto the mattress. Jean's desire was almost too much to take. Harmony appeared to be on the same page as she followed Jean into bed. Harmony climbed on top and pressed one leg between Jean's. The pressure on Jean's clit through her panties made her groan with both satisfaction and intensified lust.

Jean's hands found Harmony's ass, her fingers sliding across the silky fabric of Harmony's panties. She gripped Harmony tightly, pulling her close as Harmony began to rock in a desperate tempo that Jean's hips rose to meet. Jean lost herself in the rhythm of the motion, the press of Harmony's body on hers, rubbing against the fabric between them. The sensation was both fantastic and teasing; Jean whined and moaned as she ached for release. *So close.* Jean bit her lip and held her breath. *Oh, God.* She held Harmony's hip tight against her as a pulsing orgasm made her whole body twitch.

Harmony slowly began to push against Jean again, grinding on her. Jean watched, entranced, as Harmony rolled her hips, eyes closed, her face a portrait of longing and pleasure. Jean reached back, unhooked Harmony's bra, and pulled it off before guiding one breast up so that she could put her mouth over Harmony's hard, pink nipple. When she flicked her tongue against it, Harmony groaned and moved her hips faster.

Encouraged, Jean continued to use her tongue on and around Harmony's nipple, enjoying the feeling of it in her mouth and the sounds it elicited from Harmony. *I could do this all night.* Jean felt herself getting aroused again.

When Harmony came, she gasped and fell to the bed, panting and grinning. She kissed Jean, lightly biting her bottom lip, fueling the fire of desire inside Jean.

We're not done yet. Jean smiled as she rolled Harmony to her back. Jean pulled off her panties and straddled Harmony's hips. She bent her head to lick and suck at Harmony's nipples as she guided Harmony's fingers toward her slit.

"Oh shit, you are so wet," Harmony sighed. "God, that's hot."

"Fuck me," Jean begged, pressing closer to Harmony's hand. She felt Harmony's fingers push inside of her, and she moaned. Jean leaned back, shifting so that Harmony could fuck her deeper and harder. Harmony took the cue and began pumping her fingers faster. Jean rocked with Harmony's rhythm. When Harmony began to rub Jean's clit with her other hand, Jean let out a long guttural moan. She put a hand over her own breast, pinching her sensitive nipple.

"Oh God," Jean moaned. Her body was close to its limit. Like a rollercoaster climbing to the top of the track, the anticipation built and built until Jean plummeted over the edge into orgasm. She gasped and gripped Harmony's hand, holding it in place as ripples of pleasure radiated from the center of her body to the top of her head and tips of her toes, leaving her light-headed and tingling.

When Harmony slipped her fingers out, Jean shuddered. She hadn't come that hard in ages, and her every cell seemed to glow with the effect. Jean looked down at Harmony; her pale skin was covered in a sheen of sweat, her strawberry curls stuck to her face, her cheeks flushed pink. Her plump, pouting lips were turned up in a faint, blissful smile—eyes trained on Jean's face as Jean continued to examine her. Jean slowly ran her fingers down Harmony's chest, between her breasts, down across her belly, making a small circle around Harmony's navel before trailing back up.

After such a powerful orgasm, Jean should have been exhausted, but she could not get enough of touching Harmony. She was so warm and soft. Jean's let her fingers trail over Harmony's breasts. When she brushed her nipples, Harmony closed her eyes and sighed, her smile widening. Jean continued to lightly play with Harmony's nipples, teasing, until Harmony began to squirm beneath her.

Jean loved the look of desperate need on Harmony's face. Jean slid Harmony's panties down and off before gently pushing Harmony's legs apart and lowering herself between them. She spread Harmony with her fingers before dipping her head down and pressing her tongue against Harmony's clit. Harmony groaned and whined and pushed herself harder against Jean's face as Jean explored, discovering just what made Harmony squirm. She hummed against Harmony's clit as the motions of her tongue found a measured pace. Harmony's breathing grew shallow, and just when it seemed she'd stopped breathing altogether, Harmony sucked in a giant breath and screamed.

Jean lifted her head to watch as Harmony's back arched, her head thrown back, hands gripping the sheets. Harmony's breath came out in ragged gasps, and squealing moans as her body convulsed. Slowly Jean sat up and moved to lay beside Harmony. Harmony squeezed her legs closed and rolled to her side, still shaking.

"You okay there?" Jean asked.

"Oh, yeah," Harmony sighed, shivered once more, and lifted her face to look up at Jean. "Holy hell, that was amazing," she said.

"Yeah, it was," Jean agreed. "I guess we have some sexual chemistry."

"Some?" Harmony laughed. "I can't believe we just met. I've never experienced something like that the first time I was with somebody."

Jean laid back and thought. She had never done something like this at all. Aside from a couple sloppy, drunken hook-ups in college, if Jean slept with someone, it was because they were starting a relationship. And even in the best relationships, she'd never felt an instant chemical and physical connection the way she'd just felt with Harmony. But they weren't at the start of a relationship; they'd practically fucked out of spite. And it was *wonderful*. Jean couldn't wrap her mind around it.

"So, are you convinced I don't hate you now?" Harmony asked playfully.

Jean let out a short bark of laughter. "If you do, you have a very odd way of showing it," she said, turning her head to look at Harmony, her hair falling into her face as she did.

"I am fairly odd, or so I'm told," Harmony reached out and tucked Jean's hair behind her ear. "You really are incredibly beautiful, you know that?"

Jean shrugged; she believed that Harmony found her attractive, but she still wondered if Harmony could see that she was more than that.

"Tell me more about yourself, Jean," Harmony said as if reading her mind.

"What do you want to know?" Jean asked.

"Everything. Anything."

"Anything?" Jean thought. Her mind ran through all their previous interactions before this, to things she'd thought but not said. "You said you got your name because your parents are music nerds, right?"

"Mostly my mom, but yeah," Harmony agreed.

"Well, my parents are geeks. I'm named after Jean-Luc Picard. Jean Lucy, it doesn't sound much like *Jean-Luc*, but it's pretty obvious if you look at it on paper."

"Seriously?" Harmony began to laugh; she wrapped an arm around Jean and pulled her into a sweet embrace as her shoulders continued to shake with laughter. "That's the best thing I've ever heard."

"I told you my parents were geeks; I was born into this fannish world," Jean said, cuddling up in Harmony's arms, her head resting on Harmony's soft bosom. Harmony's laughter faded off.

"I am so jealous," Harmony said softly, her voice reverberating through her chest on which Jean's head lay. "I begged my parents to take me to conventions back when I was a kid, and they always refused. Back then, I only knew about the big commercial ones. Those are so expensive. A 'pointless waste of money' according to my dad. If I had known about the smaller fan-run ones… I don't know. I probably still wouldn't have been allowed to stay in the hotel and all, but I at least could have come for the day…" Harmony trailed off.

"I got lucky, I guess," Jean mused. "But I'm the only one of my siblings who thinks so. My brother and sister stopped going to cons as soon as they were old enough to stay home alone. My sister would still stop by now and then if the guest of honor was particularly good, but she couldn't keep up the level of interest to be worth those occasional bad interactions."

"What bad interactions?" Harmony asked.

"You know, the 'gatekeeping' I accused you of the other night. Those little tests… One time this guy began giving her shit for… oh, I don't even know what, but she completely lost it." Jean sighed. It was an unhappy memory. When they were little, her sister had been her best friend; they had so much fun running around together, playing games, and raiding the consuite for candy. But they'd drifted apart as teens, and when Kira stopped attending conventions, the distance between them became uncrossable. Jean never found a way to close the gap and get her friend back.

"That's terrible," Harmony said. "But what about your brother?"

"Oh, Will?" Jean waved her hand dismissively. "He became obsessed with basketball and basically didn't do anything else in his free time; he was never good enough to go pro, but it helped get him into Dartmouth, so I suppose it paid off. He's an ophthalmologist now."

"Neat. I appreciate the existence of ophthalmologists; I'm practically blind without my contacts," Harmony chirped. "And what about you, Jean Lucy? What do you do?"

"I'm a software engineer," Jean said.

"What kind of software?" Harmony asked.

"Right now, I'm at a company that produces language education software," Jean answered. "But what I'm doing could apply to many other types of software."

"I have to know some very particular programming for my job," Harmony said. "I'm glad I don't have to do it all the time. It can get so annoying since we do so much by committee. Other people can be so stupid."

"Yes, yes, they can," Jean agreed.

"We were acting pretty stupid earlier, weren't we?" Harmony smiled sardonically at her.

Jean smiled back. "Yes, we were." She snuggled closer to Harmony. "But if that's what it took to end up here, I think it's forgivable. Don't you?"

Harmony kissed her forehead. "Absolutely."

Chapter 19: Harmony

Harmony spent hours laying naked with Jean, talking about their jobs and lives. They had much more in common than Harmony would have ever expected. Jean was not only beautiful and smart, she was also fun and interesting. The way she told stories of ineffective coworkers made Harmony laugh and wish that her colleagues had half the wit Jean possessed.

Eventually, the conversation circled back to the convention and their mutual attraction to Christina Darlington. Harmony wouldn't admit it yet, but she was secretly glad Christina had mixed up the room keys. As hot as Christina was, it was doubtful that her intellect could compare to Jean's. *Could I have stayed up talking with Christina until the wee hours of the morning?* It seemed highly unlikely.

"Christina was my first ever girl-crush, you know," Harmony said, thinking back on those teenage days. "I can clearly remember that feeling of 'oh shit, I think I might not be straight' and the ensuing panic."

"Yeah?"

"Yeah, I was so confused for a while. Up until that point, the available data indicated that I was straight, as I'd had several crushes on boys. But after Christina started giving me the warm fuzzies, I tried to look at my attraction to others more objectively. Eventually, I accepted that I'm bi with an approximately sixty-five to thirty-five balance in attraction to women and men respectively."

"Very scientific," Jean laughed.

"I like things to be rational," Harmony replied.

"Christina was my first crush, too," Jean said with a wistful sigh. "I recorded every episode she was in and watched them over and over and over, but it took a comment from my mother to get it."

"What did your mom say?" Harmony asked. Her own parents had been utterly oblivious to her orientation until told outright.

Jean cleared her throat. "It's cute how in love with that vampire girl you are," she said in a high, gruff voice. "It reminds me of when I was head-over-heels for Luke

Skywalker as a teen. But get off the TV, young lady; you are not the only one who lives in this house!"

"Oh, that sounds familiar," Harmony said with a laugh. "Minus the part where she noticed your crush. My parents just thought my obsession was obnoxious. At one point, they banned the show entirely." Harmony snorted. "That just meant I was up at two in the morning sneak-watching it instead of sleeping. It's a wonder my grades survived that stage of my *infatuation*."

"My sister thought I was obnoxious too," Jean said. "She hated that show, but I didn't care. I thought I was in *love*. I wrote so much sappy fanfic—"

"You wrote High School Bites fanfic?" Harmony sat up; she looked at Jean, whose face flushed pink. Harmony grinned back at her. "I did too!"

"Really?" Jean's eyebrows went up, her pretty face breaking out into a brilliant grin when Harmony nodded.

"I wasn't any good at it. There are reasons I'm a scientist, you know, other than curiosity about the universe. But I wrote it anyway. I even posted it online... wait," Harmony jumped out of bed, remembering that she was naked only *after* she was halfway across the room. *Oh well. We have already had sex; what's the point of modesty?* Harmony retrieved her computer from her backpack, bounced back onto the bed, and opened it up. It took a couple of minutes, but she eventually located the long-abandoned online message board where she and her fellow HSB fans swapped their poorly written stories.

"There, look, that's me," Harmony pointed to the screen at the username FranAles4EVR. "I was a big Francesca/Alessia shipper, obviously."

"Harmony, that's… that's…"

"Super dorky, I know—"

"No, *that*," Jean pointed at another username, FARout2000. "That's *me*."

"What?!" Harmony's mouth fell open; she stared at Jean in utter disbelief, her brain barely able to form coherent thoughts. "But… what? How can…? Really?"

"Yeah, I *lived* on this message board. We totally chatted; I *remember* you," Jean said, her voice registering the same shock Harmony felt. Harmony began to scroll through the site, clicking on threads, while inside her chest, a tight fluttery feeling threatened to cut off air to her lungs. She remembered that screenname for one reason in particular.

"You wrote '*Only in My Dreams*,'" Harmony whispered, her voice catching in her throat. *Only in my*

Dreams, in which Francesca and Alessia fell so sweetly in love and slept together under the stars, in which Alessia's heart was ripped apart when it was revealed that the whole thing was nothing more than a dream.

"Yeah, I did," Jean tilted her head. "Harmony, are you okay?"

Harmony realized there were tears in her eyes. She shook her head and wiped them away. "I just… I loved that story. I must have read it a dozen times, and it made me cry every time. I can't believe you wrote that." Harmony looked at Jean, trying to reconcile the beautiful woman in front of her with the faceless person for whom she'd had such reverence—the one whose writing had touched Harmony's queer teen heart and set it on fire.

"That's crazy. I mean, I knew some people said they liked it, but—" Jean began.

"Liked it? I *loved* it. It showed me all these feelings I never knew I could feel. I tried so hard to write something like it but failed miserably. I always assumed you must be an adult fan, a real writer, or something. I didn't know you were only…"

"Fourteen, I wrote that when I was fourteen," Jean said sheepishly. "It really wasn't that good."

"It was amazing; you're so talented. You should have grown up to be an author," Harmony said earnestly.

Jean snorted softly. "Maybe in *my* dream universe." She shook her head. "But that was another lifetime. I can't believe you read it at all. What a crazy coincidence."

"Yeah, crazy…" Harmony stared at Jean's face, her cheeks still pink with embarrassment, her sweet lips curled in a bashful smile. Harmony pushed the laptop away, pulled Jean close, and kissed her; Jean wrapped her arms around Harmony and kissed her back.

These kisses were different; they weren't the lustful face-sucking of two desperately horny fangirls but the tender and passionate kisses of two connected people. Two people who hadn't known what they were looking for until they found each other. This time, when Jean pulled her down, Harmony's chest burned as hot as her clit. This wasn't just some pretty girl she was lusting after; this was Jean. And Harmony wanted Jean. When their bodies came together, joy seemed to wrap them in a blanket of warmth and happiness. After Jean came, she snuggled up against Harmony and fell asleep in her arms. Harmony drifted off to sleep, contemplating the true meaning of bliss. *This has to be it.*

Chapter 20:
Jean

Jean woke up to find Harmony lying beside her, one arm flung across Jean's torso, snoring softly. Jean's bladder was screaming to be emptied, so she gingerly moved Harmony's arm aside and quietly slid out of bed. The sheets rustled as Harmony stirred but didn't wake. Jean looked at the pale, curly-haired woman and felt a warm tenderness for her. The depth of the feeling was quite at odds with the facts. They'd only just met— teenaged webchats aside—and yet somehow, Jean already felt *connected* to Harmony.

Jean shook her head and turned to the bathroom, locking herself inside. *You're just feeling emotional because she's pretty, and it's been a long time since you've slept with anybody.* As she sat in the bathroom, Jean's brain played a montage of painful past experiences—times when she'd fallen too fast, too hard, and ended up hurt.

Emily, Jordyn, Samantha, Maria. Jean recited the names of each of the women she'd once loved, remembering each heart-breaking failed relationship. *Don't do that again.* She wanted to simply enjoy the great sex and fun connections she and Harmony shared. Could she imagine developing a real relationship with Harmony? Of course she could, but that's why she *shouldn't*. Jean reminded herself that if something happened, it would be better to let it emerge slowly. *There's no such thing as love at first sight or love at first fuck.* Jean took the hopeless romantic inside her, shoved her deep into the back closet of her mind, and locked the door.

When Jean emerged from the bathroom, Harmony turned her head, her eyes fluttering open to meet Jean's. Harmony's eyes were opalescent—they never looked quite the same shade twice. In the dim morning light, they were a faded, speckled green—like sun-dried moss. Jean was standing there, naked as the day she was born, but Harmony's eyes never left her face. She smiled sleepily at Jean.

"Good morning, beautiful," Harmony said, her voice tender and sweet. Jean's cheeks warmed, and her heart skipped a beat. Jean wanted nothing more than to slip back under the covers with Harmony and kiss her silly. She glanced at the clock. 11:21. *Shit.*

"It's a lot later than I realized," Jean said as she began to gather up her clothes.

"What's the rush?" Harmony asked, sitting up in bed, letting the sheets fall to her waist, exposing her full, soft breasts and perky pink nipples. Jean unconsciously licked her lips. The desire to touch Harmony, to taste her, made Jean's body ache. But she fought it and instead focused on the task of locating her clothing—there wasn't much of it.

"I need to check out by noon," Jean explained, locating and yanking up her shorts.

"But you're going to come back, right?" Harmony asked, eyes big with hopeful expectation.

"I'd like to, I just… I don't know what I'll do with my things," Jean thought about her suitcase, and the time it would take to pack it all up. She'd assumed she'd go home after she checked out. She'd pictured it that way in her mind.

"Bring them back here! I'm staying another night; you can leave your stuff in my room all day if you'd like," Harmony chirped. She crawled to the end of the bed and knelt on the mattress in front of Jean. She put her hands on Jean's hips, her fingers warm against Jean's bare midriff. Jean's skin tingled all over, and she could no longer resist the desire to touch Harmony.

Taking Harmony's face in her hands, Jean bent and kissed her, lightly at first, but when Harmony's tongue brushed questioningly against Jean's lips, Jean gave in and kissed her with the hunger and desire she'd been trying to suppress. The next thing she knew, she was on Harmony's lap, straddling her, kissing her like nothing else in the world mattered other than Harmony's plump, delicious lips.

Harmony's hands wandered up Jean's back, and Jean could feel her nipples harden. *You don't have time. Do you want to get charged for late check-out?*

"Mmm, no, I need to pack." Jean pulled away. Harmony whimpered in protest, but she dropped her hands and let Jean climb out of her lap and off the bed. Harmony got out of bed. She stood, stretching her shoulders, her bare chest rising as she yawned. Jean felt the desire to touch her welling up again and quickly diverted her eyes from Harmony's beautiful nakedness.

Speaking of nakedness… Jean picked up her corset and looked at it with distaste. She didn't want to go through the whole process of putting it on again, not first thing in the morning. But without it, how would she manage the "walk of shame" back to her own room?

"Hey, Harmony," Jean asked tentatively. "Is there any chance I could borrow a t-shirt? Just to get me to my room. I don't want to wear this." She held up the bodice.

"Yeah, no problem. Here." Harmony picked up a shirt and tossed it at Jean so fast that Jean didn't have time to react. It hit her square in the face.

"Oof, hey," Jean laughed. "You could have just handed it to me."

"Oops, my bad," Harmony said with a playful lilt.

Jean pulled it over her head. *Mmmmmm.* It smelled like Harmony. "I'll get it back to you in just a few minutes, as soon as I check out," Jean said, pushing her hair out of her face.

"Don't worry about it. It looks better on you anyway." Harmony had donned a t-shirt and panties. She looked so damn cute.

"Okay, I should really go," Jean said, knowing it was true but still unable to get her feet to move toward the door.

Harmony hopped over to her and landed a quick kiss on her lips. "It's okay. This isn't goodbye," Harmony said brightly. "I'll see you soon."

"Right, see you soon," Jean agreed. She kissed Harmony one more time before walking out.

Chapter 21:
Harmony

Sunday, 11:45am

While Jean was gone packing, Harmony popped out to the consuite for a bite of food, then went back to her room to tidy up. As she was rummaging through her duffle, she spotted the bright yellow fabric of her swimsuit. *It is con Sunday after all.* She pulled out the suit and looked at it. It was a one-piece retro-style suit, yellow with white polka dots. Harmony *loved* it. Yellow wasn't usually her color, but the bright, cheerful hue was perfect for wearing at a beach or pool, and the retro cut made Harmony feel like a pinup model.

Would Jean be interested in going to the hot tub? Harmony looked at her watch. *Is Jean even really coming back?* Harmony's gut said yes to both questions, and she changed into her suit.

When Jean returned and saw Harmony in her suit, her eyes went wide, although it was hard to tell whether the expression indicated surprise or appreciation of the view.

"Are you sure it's okay for me to leave my stuff here?" Jean asked when she'd recovered.

"Of course! Why wouldn't it be?" Harmony assured her.

"You look like you might… have plans," Jean said, gesturing to Harmony's swim attire.

"Getting in a final relaxing trip to the hot tub on the last day of the convention is a tradition of mine," Harmony explained. "I was hoping you'd go with me."

Jean's expression was skeptical, unsure. She looked at Harmony; there was definitely lust in her eyes; Harmony could tell by how Jean licked her lips and let her gaze linger on Harmony's curves. Jean glanced at her suitcase then back at Harmony.

"You didn't neglect to pack a swimsuit, did you?" Harmony asked pointedly, putting a hand on her hip and looking Jean straight in the eye.

"No, I packed one," Jean admitted. "But I never use it."

"Then why do you pack it?"

"Just in case?" Jean shrugged. "I suppose it's mostly habit; I'm fairly rigid about my packing habits."

"Well, this is the 'just in case' you've been waiting for," Harmony said. "Come on, doesn't seeing me in my suit make you want to go get wet together?" She gestured to her sexy swimwear.

"Seeing you in that just makes me want to take it off you again," Jean said. She stepped closer and ran a delicate finger along the edge of the suit, following the strap up and over Harmony's shoulder to where it tied behind her neck.

"Oh no," Harmony clapped her hand over Jean's before she could untie the suit. "I want to swim first. Come on. Get changed. Then *after* I can let you peel this thing off my soaking wet body." Harmony gave Jean her very best pout, and Jean sighed with a pout of her own.

"Fine," she said, turning with a huff and disappearing into the bathroom. When she reappeared, Jean was wearing a simple—and very small—black string bikini. Harmony's breathing grew shallow as her eyes took Jean in, all of her; her long bare legs, the tiny strings tied at her hips, her smooth, flat torso, the handful of breast in each black fabric triangle, it all looked so very *touchable*. Harmony couldn't help herself; she put her hands around Jean's waist, pulled her close, and kissed her. Jean kissed her back, but when Harmony's hand wandered up to cup one perfect breast, Jean smacked it away.

"I thought we were going to the hot tub," Jean scolded with a teasing lilt to her voice. Harmony whined like a lost pup when Jean stepped out of her embrace. Laughing, Jean turned and strode off toward the door. Harmony quickly snatched up her room key and rushed to catch up. Jean looked so incredibly hot as she walked down the hall, scantily clad with a smile that was half embarrassment and half mischief.

Harmony wanted to get her alone, draw her in and kiss her again. But when the elevator doors closed, leaving them standing alone, Jean made the first move. She put her hand on the back of Harmony's neck and guided it close until their lips came together in a flurry of deep, tongue-devouring kisses. When the elevator dinged and the doors began to open, Jean pulled away instantly, leaving Harmony dizzy and tingling. *Oy vey. What made me want to leave the room again?*

Harmony's bare feet slapped quietly on the tile as she followed Jean across the pool deck to the jacuzzi. There were three other people — a man and two women — already lounging in the hot water. Disappointment numbed the excited tingling in Harmony's chest. There was still plenty of room for them to sit comfortably in the water, but the presence of others precluded any *naughty* behavior.

"Hello," Harmony greeted them with friendly cheer, even as her internal monologue begged them to fuck off. They greeted her back.

"Harmony, right?" The man asked by way of greeting.

"That's me," Harmony said as she eased herself into the hot water and tried to recall the man's name. *Peter? Right? Maybe?* She didn't dare guess aloud.

"We were on that 'Ask a Scientist' panel together last year," he reminded her. Harmony nodded, the memory floating hazily to the forefront of her mind. She was no surer of his name, but it helped.

"Oh yeah, totally, you're into astronomy, right?" Harmony asked. The man nodded. Harmony and Jean settled into seats across the jacuzzi from the trio. Harmony chatted amiably with Maybe-Peter about the cosmos and her job and his related hobbies until she noticed that Jean wasn't saying anything. *You're here to be with her. Shut your trap for once.*

Harmony tried to casually disengage from the conversation, but she was terrible at it. When people talked to her, she had a natural inclination to talk back, often at length.

One of the women complimented Harmony's swimsuit and asked where she'd gotten it, which led to a whole new discussion of swimwear and hard-to-fit body types. Harmony had found the suit online. It was hard to find ones that fit her large chest. The media would have one believe that having big boobs is an advantage, but most of the clothing industry seemed to think making anything above a C-cup was just not worth their time.

"You're so quiet," Harmony said to Jean when the conversation finally died down, and their tub companions began to head out.

"I didn't have much to contribute," Jean said softly but with a hint of bitterness in her voice. Harmony tilted her head and scrutinized Jean's face. Harmony would have found Jean's expression impassive and difficult to read a day ago, but she felt like she knew her better now. She'd seen a wide range of emotions cross Jean's pretty features as they'd talked and fucked on and off all night. Jean was unhappy.

"Are you okay?" Harmony asked.

"I'm fine," Jean was clearly lying. Harmony raised a disbelieving eyebrow at her, and she sighed. "Fine, I guess I felt a little left out, and it's hard for my mind not to spin on things I don't like about myself when that happens."

"What could there possibly be not to like about you?" Harmony asked, incredulous. In her eyes, Jean was perfect by every definition. But Jean only shook her head. Harmony slid closer and pulled Jean onto her lap. Immersed in water, Jean was as light as a feather, and Harmony lifted her with ease. Jean allowed herself to picked-up; she wrapped her arms around Harmony's neck and smiled faintly at her.

"Everything I know about you, I like," Harmony said, kissing Jean lightly. "Except maybe that part where you thought I hated you. But I'll forgive it because I was acting like a bit of an ass earlier."

"Thanks," Jean said, returning Harmony's brief, soft kiss. "I like you too."

"Good." Harmony kissed Jean again, letting her lips linger until Jeans' mouth opened, and their kisses grew frantic and hungry once more. Harmony squirmed with desire as her tongue danced with Jean's, the taste of chlorine mixing with their kisses as Jean pulled her closer, sending a wave of water to splash against Harmony's chest and neck. Under the water, Harmony ran one had along Jean's bare back, feeling the ridges of her spine; the other hand she slipped between the gap in Jean's thighs. Harmony flicked her fingers, brushing them against the fabric of Jean's suit, between her legs. Jean whimpered and clamped her thighs together, trapping Harmony's hand in place. Harmony twitched her fingers again, pushing them against Jean, rubbing at the spandex that separates her from Jean's sensitive flesh. Jean groaned and, after a few more flicks, reached down and pulled Harmony's hand out and away from her groin.

"We're in a public pool," Jean whispered against Harmony's lips.

"Technically, it's a private pool, owned and operated by—" Harmony was cut off by a deep kiss from Jean. She moved her hand, the one that had been exiled from Jean's crotch, to cover Jean's breast. She squeezed Jean lightly through her suit and felt Jean squirm in her arms again. Harmony let two fingers sneak beneath the fabric to tease Jean's nipple; Jean gasped, and it took all of Harmony's self-control not to pull the suit aside and continue the exploration with her tongue.

God, I want to suck on her tits. Oh my God, why are we at the pool?

"Should we maybe go back to my room?" Harmony asked, and Jean nodded in fervent agreement.

"Yes, let's go, please," she pleaded, her voice high and tight with desire.

It was hard to break the series of kisses, but Harmony pulled back and let Jean off her lap. Jean stepped out of the water, and Harmony sighed deeply at the view of Jean's backside, dripping with water, her suit threatening to ride all the way up into her perfect little ass. Harmony wanted to reach between her legs, grab her, pull aside her suit, and get the full view of Miss Jean Lucy from the back. But instead, she reached out for Jean's hand and climbed out after her.

Goosebumps spread across Harmony's skin as the cool air hit her wet body. She and Jean scampered over to retrieve towels, drying as quickly as possible to stave off more heat-sucking evaporation.

"You're so sexy," Jean said, seemingly out of the blue as Harmony squeezed water from the ends of her curls.

"Right back atcha," Harmony grinned. Jean shook her head and then shivered violently. "Come on, let's get back upstairs," said Harmony, grabbing Jean's hand once more. She pulled her from the pool deck, down the freezing cold corridor to the elevator. This time a family was in the elevator car with them, so they stood, chastely holding hands, until they reached their floor, where Harmony took off toward her room at almost a run, dragging Jean laughing behind her.

As soon as the door to the hotel room closed behind them, Harmony pulled her in and kissed her deeply, their lips parting so that their tongues could meet. Jean let out a satisfied groan, like someone dying of thirst who had just found water.

After a few minutes of ravenous kissing, Harmony backed off slightly, teasing Jean. Jean whimpered as their lips brushed lightly, then parted, a hair's breadth away. Jean leaned forward, but Harmony pulled back again, enjoying the sounds her teasing elicited from Jean. She lightly ran her tongue along Jean's bottom lip but did not kiss her, not yet. Jean whined and squirmed in Harmony's arms, pushing their bodies together. Finally, Harmony gave in, and their mouths came together in a string of hungry kisses that left them breathless and gasping.

As they kissed, Harmony's fingers began to trace along the edge of Jean's bikini top, down from her shoulder, slowly running along her smooth skin just inside the edges of the damp fabric, toward the soft curve just under her breast. Harmony slipped her fingers inside the suit and pulled it aside. The skin of Jean's small round breast was prickled with goosebumps, and her nipple stood erect, pink and perfect and just *begging* to be sucked. Harmony could not resist; she cupped her hand under the soft mound of flesh and bent her head, covering Jean's nipple with her mouth. She sucked lightly, flicking her tongue with zealous enthusiasm as Jean moaned encouragingly. Harmony could never get enough of Jean's breasts; she could spend all day running her tongue across every little bump of her areola like she *belonged* in Harmony's mouth. She squeezed Jean with her hand as she sucked harder, her teeth grazing Jean's sensitive skin.

"Oh, God," Jean breathed, and Harmony hummed with pleasure. Jean grabbed Harmony's hair and pulled her up for another series of feverish kisses. Harmony pushed aside the other side of Jean's bikini and caressed her left breast as they kissed. She could feel Jean's nipple hard against her palm as she massaged her. She pressed against it, rubbing the sensitive nub with the flat of her hand as she squeezed. *God, she has the most amazing boobs.* Harmony pulled back from Jean's kisses to replace her palm with her mouth. She circled her nipple with her tongue before lightly biting it. Jean gasped, and Harmony wondered if she was maybe giving Jean's nipples *too much* attention.

"Is this okay?" she asked, lifting her head. Jean smiled wickedly at her.

"Oh, yes. Although I am starting to go a little weak in the knees... And your body is far too covered up."

"Is that so? How do you suppose we solve these dilemmas?" Harmony asked with her own mischievous grin.

Jean slowly backed away; she slid onto the bed and laid back, her eyes never leaving Harmony's. "Take it off," she commanded.

Harmony decided to play it difficult. She removed her watch. "There, I took *it* off," she teased as she set the timepiece down on the dresser.

Jean narrowed her eyes at Harmony, lips pursed in mock anger. "You *know* what I meant," she said.

"Ooooh, this?" Harmony asked, running her fingers along her suit, across her cleavage, up toward where it tied in the back, then away again, continuing to tease. "I don't know…"

"If that's the way you want to play it," Jean raised her eyebrows at Harmony as she began to move her suit back into place, covering her breasts.

"No! I'm taking it off!" Harmony rushed to comply as Jean laughed.

"Oh, so you like seeing my boobs then?" Jean giggled.

"*Very* much." Harmony slid her suit down and stepped out of it.

"Good," Jean said and pulled the bikini top off entirely. Harmony crawled onto the bed and pulled at Jean's bottoms; Jean lifted her hips to allow Harmony to slide them off.

"Much better," Harmony climbed on top of Jean. She tried to slide her leg between Jean's, but their cool, damp post-pool skin stuck together.

"Hmm, we have a bit of a friction problem here," Harmony cursed the properties of water as she rolled off to Jean's side.

"Well, there's one place where I'm sure friction will be.*no* problem." Jean took Harmony's hand and guided it between her legs until Harmony's fingers found her slick wetness.

"Mmmm, I like *this* place," Harmony whispered as she ran her fingers up and down Jean's slit, spreading her natural lubricant up to her clit. Jean moaned in approval as Harmony stroked the most sensitive part of her body. Harmony leaned forward so that she could lick and suck on Jean's nipple, but she kept most of her focus on her hand as she played with Jean's clit, enjoying the feeling of that slick little button under her fingers and reveling in the sound of Jean's moans of pleasure. She didn't stop until Jean came, crying out and clamping her thighs shut as she did; she rolled to her side, shaking with the effect of her orgasm. Harmony curled up behind her, content.

Chapter 22:
Jean

Sunday, 12:30pm

Jean and Harmony changed back into their clothes as casually as they'd know each other forever. The familiarity of it caused questions to tickle at the back of Jean's mind. *Why is this so comfortable?* It didn't make sense. And yet, it *was* comfortable.

Once dressed, Jean did her best to dry her damp swimsuit with the blow dryer so that she could pack it back in her suitcase.

"You're so organized and neat," Harmony commented, eyeballing Jean's open suitcase.

"And you're so not," Jean teased, nudging the yellow suit Harmony had left in a lump on the floor.

"Yeah, but I can be," Harmony grinned as she picked up the discarded swimwear. "I just need to have a reason to be." She hung the suit up to dry in the bathroom. "And you're a pretty good reason."

"Me?"

"Yeah, you know. I'd clean up for you. Ask my roommate, I am capable of tidiness. Maybe not as organized as you though," Harmony said, gesturing at Jean's suitcase. "It looks like you packed for every possible contingency."

"I tried, but this convention has taken some seriously unexpected turns," Jean remarked as she zipped her suitcase shut and set it on the floor.

"Yeah, no kidding," Harmony pushed damp curls out of her face and grinned up at Jean. "I came here expecting standard con shenanigans and hoping to hook-up with Christina, but instead I fell for you."

"Oh," Jean's heart thumped heavily in her chest, suddenly heavy with the weight of unwanted emotion. *'Fell for you'?* A tingle went up Jean's spine and she straightened her back. *What does that mean?*

"What're you thinking?" Harmony asked, tilting her head. "Your expression just super changed."

"I... I just..." Jean stammered. "I should be getting home."

"Already?" Harmony protested with a pout that made something twitch inside of Jean. She didn't want to disappoint Harmony. Her insides twisted into knots at the thought of making Harmony unhappy. And that was why she had to leave. Now.

"Yes. I, uh, I have work tomorrow," Jean wheeled her bag out of the room, Harmony hot on her heels.

"I wish you would stay. There's still some clean up work to be done and then there's the 'dead dog' party." As they rode the elevator down, Harmony explained the JanCon tradition of closing up shop and then capping it off with one last round of drinking and socializing and, inevitably, games. They could stay up all night again; Harmony was planning to. That's why she had kept her hotel room for one extra day.

"That sounds like fun, but I really should go home. I need to do laundry and…" Jean shrugged and looked down at her phone; she watched as the little icon that was her Lyft began to wiggle. She couldn't look at Harmony. The pleading look on her face was too persuasive.

"Okay, but before you go, there's something I need to tell you," Harmony said. She put a hand on Jean's cheek and Jean was forced to look into those gold-flecked eyes, so earnestly trained on hers. "I think I'm falling in love with you," Harmony said, and the bottom fell out of Jean's stomach.

"You can't know that," Jean protested, her voice coming out in a soft gush of air; it was as if the shock Harmony's words made Jean's lungs forget how to breathe properly. "You can't be falling in love with me; you just met me."

"I know, but…" Harmony's mouth worked silently for a moment before she sighed and ran her thumb across Jean's cheek. "I am; I'm falling in love with you. Honestly, I'm pretty sure I love you already. It's not a feeling I often experience and it's unmistakable. I fell in love with you last night."

"You fell in *bed* with me last night," Jean said, pulling away.

"No, it wasn't that," Harmony replied stubbornly. "It was after all of that. I felt it when we were talking, when I found out who you are." Harmony was insistent.

Who I am? "You don't really know me," Jean said, lifting her head against the mounting anxiety in her chest. "And I don't really know you, Harmony."

"So, get to know me. Date me. Let's take this beyond the confines of the con." Harmony implored. When Jean didn't answer Harmony's voice took on a pleading tone. "Please, Jean. Be my girlfriend."

"Girlfriend?" Jean squeaked. "We *just met.*"

"So?"

"So, we just met. We don't have anything in common—"

"We have *everything* in common!" Harmony interrupted.

She had a point, but Jean couldn't concede it. She shook her head. "We live on opposite sides of the city," she said weakly.

Harmony wasn't buying that either, she rolled her hazel eyes and pursed her plump lips. "You said you live in the middle," Harmony pointed out. "So, we can't really be on opposite sides then, can we?"

It was solid reasoning. Jean couldn't refute that. She searched her brain for some now excuse but all she found there was a blank white nothingness—a void. She could feel panic and anxiety seeping into every cell in her body. *What do I say? What do I do?*

"I don't, I can't…" Jean paused, the panic rising like a swelling tide in her chest. She shook her head as if shaking it could shake all of it away. "You can't just say you're in love with me, that's too much," Jean said. She pushed open the hotel door and stepped out into the gray spring evening air.

Harmony followed. "Too much what?" Harmony asked sincerely. She was being so open and honest, Jean couldn't take it.

"Pressure!" she all but yelled. "Harmony, it's too much pressure!"

"I'm sorry, I'm not trying to pressure you. Take all the time you need-"

"No, you don't understand," Jean shook her head. "I can't be in a relationship with you,"

"Why not?" Harmony asked. She already looked hurt.

You're not doing this to hurt her. Why are you doing this? "Because I can't start dating somebody who already thinks they love me," Jean said with calm logic that surprised even herself. That was it, wasn't it? Jean had gone through too many relationships that had escalated too rapidly and done too much emotional damage. This depth of feeling that Harmony was expressing was like a warning written in bright, blinking neon lights. *If we had a relationship and it failed, it would hurt so much. It would tear me apart.*

"I'm sorry, I have a bad habit of being overly-honest—" Harmony began.

"Harmony…" Jean interrupted, although she didn't know what to say. Silence hung between them. The wind softly pushed on Harmony's curls, which almost looked more blonde than red in the diffuse gray light. *She's so beautiful.* Jean had to resist the urge to reach out and touch Harmony. *We're saying goodbye. Not see you later. Goodbye.* Jean looked away, letting her eyes rest on the handle of her suitcase.

"Can you forget I said it?" Harmony pleaded softly. Jean shook her head and Harmony took Jean's hand left and held it between both of hers. "I won't say it again, just give me a chance," Harmony begged.

"Even if you don't say, it I'll know that's how you feel. I'll know. I'll see it every time you look at me." Jean looked at Harmony again. The affection and attachment in Harmony's eyes made the panic inside of Jean jump into overdrive. She pulled her hand away. "Please don't. Don't look at me like that."

"Like what?" Harmony asked, light eyebrows knitted.

"Like you…" *Like you love me.* Jean couldn't even get the words out now. The air felt thick and hard to breathe, Jean's brain fogged as if deprived of oxygen. "I'm sorry," she whispered. It was all she could say.

Jean sat down on the bench along the exterior of the building. Harmony sat next to her. She didn't touch her or even look at her. She just sat there. Jean wanted to forget that she was there. She pulled out her phone and unlocked it with trembling fingers. *Where is that Lyft?* It was seconds away. Jean craned her neck to look up and down the street until she saw the black Honda Civic pull into the hotel's drive. Jean stood and Harmony followed suit.

"Can I at least get your number?" Harmony asked as the Lyft driver hefted Jean's suitcase into the trunk.

"I don't think that's a good idea," Jean said.

"But—"

"Goodbye, Harmony," Jean looked into Harmony's eyes one last time. "It was really wonderful to get to know you this weekend. I wish you all the best."

"You too," Harmony said sadly.

Jean planted on last light kiss on Harmony's full lips before she turned and climbed into the Lyft.

Chapter 23: Harmony

How did I manage to fall in love and get my heart broken in one weekend? Harmony wondered wistfully as she watched Jean's Lyft drive away. The pain in her chest was surprisingly acute. Harmony didn't believe in fate or in love at first sight, and somehow, as she stood there, Harmony suddenly had a lot more sympathy for Romeo and Juliette. *O, wilt thou leave me so unsatisfied, Jean?*

Pining like this, with her heart burning and her mind swimming, wasn't familiar to her. Falling rapidly in love wasn't something she did. That wasn't the type of thing that happened to Harmony. But it was a not-uncommon occurrence for somebody else she knew. *Gabby.*

Harmony found her long-time friend and immediately wrapped her in a hug. Gabby reeled in surprise but caught herself and hugged Harmony back.

"What's going on, Harm?" she asked.

"She's gone…" Harmony whispered, unexpected tears springing to her eyes.

"Who's gone?" Gabby pulled back, hands on Harmony's shoulders, and looked her over. "Are you crying?"

"Jean. She left, and she doesn't want to see me again and wouldn't even give me her number," Harmony said, her voice rough and squeaky with the effort of holding back her tears.

"The cosplayer?"

Harmony nodded. "We ended up together last night, and then we talked and I… I..." Harmony took several gasping breaths. "I fell in love with her." The dam inside her broke, and Harmony began to cry. Harmony hated crying; it was an illogical, stupid chemical reaction to stimulus. But she couldn't stop.

"Oh, sweety." Gabby pulled Harmony back into her arms and rubbed her back as she cried. "You didn't tell her that, did you?" All Harmony could do in response was cry harder. She felt Gabby's body shake with quiet laughter.

"Oh, my sweet summer child," Gabby chuckled. "You can't tell a girl you love her after one night. That's some turbo-speed ultra-lesbian shit right there."

On some level, Harmony knew Gabby was right. Falling in love in one night made zero sense. It wasn't really one night, though. Harmony had come to terms with the fact that she'd been hot on Jean since the moment she saw her. It wasn't love at first sight, not love at the speed of light...

"More like warp nine," Harmony said aloud, her sobs melting away into whimpers.

"Huh?" Gabby pulled back to stare at Harmony again. Harmony sniffed and wiped tears from her cheeks.

"I was just thinking; I don't believe in love at first sight, but if 'love at first sight' is equivalent to love at the speed of light, this, what I feel, is like love at warp nine-point-nine. And I think I can believe in that."

"TOS nine-point-nine or Next Gen?" Gabby asked and Harmony scowled at her.

"I think you get my point," Harmony said. She'd obviously meant Next Gen. They were talking about Jean Lucy, after all.

"Well, I think maybe you should slow to impulse next time before blurting things out. Telling somebody you love them that quick is liable to scare them off," Gabby lectured.

"Well, I know that *now*," Harmony said with a deep sigh. "What am I going to do? I know she liked me. I know it. But she wouldn't even give me her number! Should I Google her or—"

"You scared her off once, I don't think stalking her is your answer," Gabby pointed out.

"But what if I never see her again?" Harmony felt tears once again threatening to spill from her eyes and she blinked them away. "I really think she liked me back. We connected."

"Okay, so let her Google *you*," Gabby said with a shrug. "If she really did like you then maybe she'll regret leaving you hanging and look you up."

"You think she'll do that?" Harmony asked hopefully.

"I wouldn't hang my hopes on it, but the probability is certainly greater than zero." Gabby had a point. Greater than zero wasn't zero.

"Thanks, Gabby," Harmony gave Gabby one more quick hug. "I don't know what I would have done if you hadn't been here this weekend. In a purely selfish way, I'm kind of glad Tam dumped you."

"Oh, I'm so glad the demise of my two-year long relationship could serve to help you get over your two day long tragic love story," Gabby said, her voice dripping with sarcasm.

"I'm sorry. I have been so wrapped up in Christina and then Jean that I have barely asked about how you're doing with the whole Tammy thing." Harmony ducked her head sheepishly.

Gabby waved her hand dismissively and smiled at Harmony. "That's okay," she said. "I didn't really want to talk about it. Your little drama has been a pretty good distraction, actually."

"I was pretty dramatic, huh?" Harmony chuckled uncomfortably.

"I can't say that I've ever seen you like that, so yeah. Dramatic would be a good descriptor." Gabby tittered.

"I need a distraction. Jean has invaded my whole mind, heart, and lady-bits." Harmony shifted her hips side to side. "She's got me all squirmy. I need to get my mind off her. I think I should stop standing here talking about her and go help with take-down."

"That sounds like a good plan," Gabby agreed.

"Want to join me?" Harmony asked.

"Naw, I gotta get headed home soon," Gabby replied, pointing a thumb in the direction of the hotel's front door.

"You're not going to stay for the Dead Dog party?" Harmony asked.

"Nope."

"Aw, bummer. I guess I'll have to get my cuddles elsewhere…" Harmony considered for a moment. "Maybe Chris is up for a little casual hook-up. Making out with a man might help me shake this lovesick feeling."

"Have fun with that," Gabby said with a shake of her head. Gabby didn't understand life on the 'bi-cycle'—tapping into her straight side for a bit could actually help Harmony get Jean out of her system. The more she thought about it the more she liked the idea.

"I will have fun, so there." Harmony stuck her tongue out at Gabby. After a brief hug the two parted ways. Harmony made her way back to the consuite where she found Chris busy cleaning and packing away the bar equipment.

"Need a hand?" Harmony asked.

"Always!" Chris beckoned her over and they both got to work together turning the space from a consuite and bar back into a hotel suite.

"Hey, when we're done with this, wanna make out for a while?" Harmony asked Chris as they pulled tape and plastic sheeting up from the floor.

"Of course! How could I say no to an offer like that? Kissing cute girls is pretty much my favorite activity." Christ wiggled his eyebrows. "Outside of sex with cute girls, that is."

"Well, that's not happening," Harmony said firmly. "But I could use a little physical comfort."

"I thought you were feeling the ladies these days." Christ said and Harmony sighed in exasperation.

"I was, and now I am missing the feel of stubble scraping off a layer of my skin. Want to second guess the offer again?" She put a hand on her hip and looked at him.

"Nope, nope! Sorry. I'm in, I'm in," Chris said hastily. "Hey everybody, I wanna make out with this cute girl. So, if we could all work a little faster— ow, hey!" Chris jumped back when Harmony smacked him in the arm and flashed her a shit-eating grin.

Harmony shook her head and laughed. She liked that Chris was chill and fun. She knew he could kiss well and would do so without catching feelings for her. *Unlike me and Jean.* Harmony pushed away thoughts of

Jean and got down to the business of cleaning out the ConSuite. She wanted that distraction; she needed it.

Chapter 24:
Jean

Jean arrived at her apartment filled with uncertainty and regret. *How did I let her get under my skin? How do I have this many feelings about a woman I just met?* She set down her keys and wheeled her suitcase into her bedroom. There was pressure at the back of her throat and behind her eyes like she was close to crying, but she knew she wouldn't actually cry.

Jean tried to ignore it and begin her unpacking routine, but the feeling wouldn't leave. Her breath came harder. *No, no, no,* she repeated to herself, struggling to make herself keep moving. She dropped her toiletry kit, and it fell, clattering as the contents spilled out onto her bathroom floor. She looked at her hands; they were shaking. Her whole body was shaking. She forced out a small, choked cry, just to see if she could push past the panic. If she could start crying, maybe the anxiety would break with the tears.

Unable to either cry or stop shaking, Jean left the mess in the bathroom and curled up on her bed. *Why did I leave like that? Why didn't I at least entertain the possibility of a relationship with Harmony?* Of course, she had entertained the possibility. It had weighed on her mind all day. *But why didn't I tell her? What was it about her that made me want to flee?*

A deep ache throbbed in Jean's chest, and she knew why she'd run. She was protecting herself. She curled tighter into herself. Her heart felt as fragile as glass inside her ribs like the littlest thing could shatter it. She didn't want Harmony to break her heart, but in pulling it out of her reach—by protecting it against the possibility of heartbreak—she'd held on too tight and cracked it herself. Jean clutched her hands together, pushing them against her chest. A sharp pain lashed through her like she could feel the jagged edges of the crack in her heart.

No, it's just a panic attack. The sharp pain is because I'm not breathing. *Come on, Jean, breathe.* Jean forced herself to take slow, deep breaths. But the third exhale, she was crying. She cried and cried; still, the bonds of anxiety didn't break. Jean screamed into her pillow. She turned and stared at the bottle of Xanax on her nightstand. *Just take it, feel better*. But part of her screamed, "you deserve this pain. You need this because you caused it." Jean flung her arm out and knocked everything off the small bedside table. She screamed again and clenched her fists tight against her chest.

Why would Harmony want somebody as broken as me? *How could she? She doesn't know*. Jean's nails bit into her palms, and she focused on the pain. *But why not try? Why not give her a chance? The benefit of the doubt?* Jean rocked back and forth until her tears stopped, and calm resolve began to spread through her like ice water in her veins. She knew what she had to do.

I need to find Harmony. She needed to try. Maybe it wouldn't amount to anything; maybe Harmony would turn away from her like everybody else did. *But maybe she won't. What if she is as genuine as she seems?*

Panic rose in Jean once again, but it wasn't the crippling, internal pain this time. It was a frantic sense of urgency—a need to move and do things. I need to go back. I need to go back now. Jean jumped out of bed, muscles twitching with anticipation. Jean's urgent need to return to JanCon and to Harmony made the idea of waiting unthinkable. The thought of calling for a Lyft or circling the block for parking made her insides itch. It she didn't move, she would go out of her skin. She jammed her feet into her sneakers, yanked her coat off the hook, and was out the door.

Jean strode briskly along the cold, windy sidewalk street. *It's not far; I'll be there soon.*She wanted to run, but she didn't want to look as panicked as she felt. She'll still be there. *I don't need to rush*, Jean tried to tell herself. But when she turned the corner and saw the hotel, she couldn't help it. Jean burst into a sprint.

Jean didn't stop running until she was standing in the doorway of the hotel. *Where do I go from here?* She stood frozen, suddenly hyper-aware of how hard her heart was beating. It was hammering out a rhythm like an out-of-control bongo drummer on speed. She was breathing hard, too, sweat dripping down her back. She knew her face was flushed and that she probably looked like a wild, crazy mess. But she decided she didn't care; in fact, she welcomed her harried appearance. It was a side of herself that Harmony hadn't seen. And if Harmony took one look at her—strung out as she was— and walked away, that would tell Jean all she needed to know. But if she still wanted her, even in her panicked state, maybe they would have a chance.

Jean stalked toward the consuite, or what was once the consuite. Everything had been packed up; a stack of rubber tubs was the only indication that the room had once been the epicenter of JanCon.

Jean looked around. Sitting on a sofa in the middle of the room sat Harmony—lips locked with a man. Jean stopped dead.

Chapter 25: Harmony

Sunday, 4:10pm

"Harmony!" Jean's voice cut across the room, and Harmony's head whipped around, breaking the kiss she and Chris had been sharing. Jean stood in the doorway, red-faced, her hair a wind-blown mess, staring at her with a wild, frantic expression. Harmony's eyes went wide, first in surprise and then fear. The fear was like a punch to the gut. *Oh, fuck. What have I done?* It was like some sort of dream; she felt detached from the reality of it. *She came back for me and found me with him.* Harmony jumped up and away from Chris.

"Jean, this isn't what it looks like," she rushed to say; she could feel her bottom lip trembling. "I mean, I don't know what it looks like, but it isn't anything."

They stood stock-still, staring at each one another. Jean's chest heaved, her breathing heavy. *Did she run here? What does she want?* Harmony could feel her blood rushing in her ears as her pulse hammered out a frantic rhythm.

"Do you still want to date me?" Jean asked.

The question came as a shock. *Do you still want to date me?* Harmony's thoughts were muddled with emotion as the question reverberated in her head. *Do you still want to date me?* She blinked at Jean as her mind finally got a hold of itself and properly processed the question. *Do I still want to date her?* "Yes, of course, I do. Of course, I want to date you, Jean"

"Are you sure?" Jean asked taking a tentative step towards her.

Harmony nodded vigorously. "I do. Really. What I was doing, just now with Chris, that doesn't mean anything. I was just… I was trying to get over you. I'm sorry—"

"You don't have to apologize." Jean shook her head. "I don't care about that; you didn't know I was coming back, and even if you did, you don't owe me anything. I'm the one who should apologize."

"For what?" Harmony asked.

"I told you I didn't want to date you, but that was a lie." Jean looked at her feet.

"You… you *do* want to date me?" Harmony asked uncertainly.

"Only if you're sure you want to date me," Jean replied, looking up, her eyebrows knit in uncertainty. "Before you decide, you should know that I'm a crazy mess of anxiety and self-doubt. I think of every worst-case scenario and then find one worse than that. My brain spins in twelve directions at once; I'm smart to the detriment of intelligence. That doesn't make any sense, but it does to me because I'm basically a train wreck up here." Jean pointed to her temple. "That's why I ran away. I told you I have anxiety but knowing and seeing are two different things. I can be such a disaster sometimes. Are you sure you want to deal with that?"

"Yes," Harmony said without hesitation. "We made a connection this weekend. We've found something real and rare. I'm sorry if I came on too strong and triggered your anxiety—"

"Don't be sorry; it's my stupid brain," Jean interrupted.

"Hey." Harmony pulled Jean in close and pushed her hair away from her face. She put a hand on Jean's cheek. "I like your brain. I mean, I hate that it tortures you sometimes, but I love the way your mind works. I've been in awe of you since I knew you as FARout2000. You're brilliant."

"I'm really not," Jean protested.

"Yeah, you are. But we have the rest of forever to argue about that." Harmony stopped and looked up uncertainly at Jean. *The rest of forever*. Would those words trigger Jean's anxiety? Harmony crossed her fingers and hoped she hadn't put her foot in her mouth. She didn't want to scare Jean away again as quickly as she'd gotten her back.

But Jean didn't even flinch. "I hope you're right," she said. "Because I think I'm falling in love with you too." She pulled Harmony close and kissed her. Around them the other people in the consuite—who Harmony had forgotten about entirely—began to clap and cheer.

"Way to go, Harmony," Chris shouted.

Harmony turned to give him a dirty look. "Shut up, you." She pulled Jean by the hand, out of the consuite until they found a spot alone in the corner of the hallway. "I'm sorry, Jean," she said. "My friends can be a bit much."

Jean laughed. "You know, normally that would have made me melt with embarrassment. But I'm so happy you still want me, that I couldn't possibly care less."

"Really?" Harmony grinned.

"Really. Now shut up and kiss me," Jean drew her in, and Harmony melted into the kiss. There was joy, desire, and promise in that kiss. It was the best kiss Harmony had ever had at JanCon, and certainly not the last of its kind.

One year later

"Come on, Harm, let's go," Jean called from outside the bathroom door.

"What's the rush?" Harmony called back.

"I told you, I want to have the chance to see all the party rooms before we go down to the gaming floor," Jean said. "I promised Kaolin we'd be playing Zar before midnight."

Harmony opened the bathroom door. "There's plenty of time, sweetheart."

Jean's eyes went wide. "Oh my God, Harmony. You look amazing,' she gushed.

Harmony felt herself blush. "Do you really think so?"

Jean nodded with wild enthusiasm. "You look wicked sexy."

Harmony grinned. "Thanks… You know I'm still not sure how you talked me into trying on a corset in the first place," she said, running her hands along the curves of the red-and-black bodice. "Are you sure my boobs don't look too big?"

"Your boobs look *perfect*," Jean assured her. "Now come on, let's go get drunk and play games with our friends." Jean tugged at her arm, and Harmony allowed herself to be led out of their room toward the elevator.

"I like how they're 'our friends' now," Harmony said, squeezing her girlfriend's hand.

"Me too," Jean replied, squeezing back. "You know, sometimes I think about sending Christina Darlington a thank you card."

"A thank you card?" Harmony repeated, looking quizzically at Jean.

Jean nodded. "Yes. I want to tell her thank you for giving me the motivation to overcome my anxiety and come to JanCon, because without that, they wouldn't be 'our friends.' I want to thank her for that. And for you."

"For me?" Harmony feigned ignorance.

"Of course. If she hadn't switched the room keys, I wouldn't have slept with you." Jean grinned. "Duh."

Harmony giggled. "Do you ever wonder if she gave you my key on purpose?" she asked.

"The thought has occurred to me," Jean said with a nod. "I could ask her in the thank you note, but I hear she never answers fan mail."

"Too bad, I guess we'll never know for certain," Harmony said.

"I know one thing for certain." Jean touched Harmony's cheek.

"What's that?" Harmony asked although she didn't need to. She knew.

"I'm certain that I love you," Jean said.

"I'm certain that I love you too," Harmony replied before the two stepped out of the elevator to enjoy the convention together.

www.ingramcontent.com/pod-product-compliance
Lightning Source LLC
Chambersburg PA
CBHW050836190726
48286CB00007B/2110